Notes Across the Aisle

Notes Across the Aisle

Edited by Peter Carver

Thistledown Press Ltd.

Canadian Cataloguing in Publication Data
Main entry under title:

Notes across the aisle

ISBN 1-895449-45-6

1. Short stories, Canadian (English).* 2. Young adult fiction, Canadian (English).*
3. Canadian fiction (English) - 20th century.* I. Carver, Peter, 1936-

PS8329.N67 1995   C813'.01089283   C95-920164-5
PR9197.32.N67 1995

Book design by A.M. Forrie
Set in New Baskerville
by Thistledown Press
Printed and bound in Canada

Thistledown Press Ltd.
633 Main Street
Saskatoon, Saskatchewan, S7H 0J8

The Canada Council | Le Conseil des Arts
for the Arts | du Canada
since 1957 | depuis 1957

Thistledown Press gratefully acknowledges the financial assistance of the Canada
Council for the Arts, the Saskatchewan Arts Board, and the Government of Canada
through the Book Publishing Industry Development Program for
its publishing program.

Publisher's Note

Notes Across the Aisle is Thistledown Press's second anthology of short stories for young adults. *The Blue Jean Collection* (1992) was such a success, confirming the publisher's perception that there was a need for such literature and an interested readership, that a complementary anthology was a natural.

The stories in *Notes Across the Aisle* were selected from submissions to Thistledown's National Young Adult Short Story competition. Once again the publisher had the competition externally adjudicated to determine the winning story and the runner-up.

Congratulations to Linda Holeman for her winning story, "How to Tell Renata" and to Jacqueline Pinto for "Bulat Kisses" which was selected as the runner-up.

The remaining fifteen stories were chosen for inclusion in the anthology from literally hundreds of submissions to the contest.

Notes Across the Aisle will be a worthy addition to a dynamic and growing literary genre in Canadian publishing.

Thanks to all the writers who submitted their stories and made the selection such a challenge for the jury. Thanks to the jury, Pat Barclay, R.P. MacIntyre and Maria Martella for selecting the winning and runner-up stories, and thanks to Peter Carver for his editorial guidance.

It is to be hoped that this is the establishment of a tradition in the publishing of future anthologies.

Contents

Preface

Peter Carver

How to set up your life. How to make sense of relationships. How to tell the people in your world that you're *you*. How to make sense of social structures you've had no hand in creating. How to come to terms with problems, issues, *conundrums* that are beyond human resolution.

This is the stuff of *Notes Across the Aisle*, seventeen glimpses into the too-fast-growing-up mid-teen world of the 1990s.

Angst, coming to terms, facing up to reality — these are the kinds of themes the authors of these stories focus most on. Because these are the issues that, willy nilly, matter most to young adults of our time.

And, if there are worries — nagging, pervasive, insoluble worries — there are also lighter moments, just to relieve the tension.

This anthology is the result of the second national short fiction contest for young adults sponsored by Thistledown Press, and once again many of the writers of the stories published here are seeing their work in print for the first time — most notably Karin Galldin, an eighteen-year-old grade twelve student at Nepean High School in Ottawa.

Professional authors generally hold that the short story is one of the most exacting of literary forms. It is one in which Canadian writers have frequently excelled. Much must be said, a world created, in just a few pages. There is neither time nor space for superfluous detail. The imperative for the writer of short fiction is always to "cut to the car chase," while not neglecting the need to create a convincing atmosphere, characters who are believable in situations which inexorably draw the reader in.

Immerse yourself now in *Notes Across the Aisle*. Seventeen stories, with settings as diverse as a steamy Sri Lankan summer, wartime Halifax, the dinosaur badlands, a North West Company fort of 200 years ago, and a future where human contact thrives only by modem. Characters who seek to take control of their lives against a range of odds: the managing tendencies of their elders, the deadly hand of economic hardship, the despair of lost love, and the ambitions others have for them.

Through most of the stories there shines, despite the odds, a sense of the dignity and moral steadfastness of the human spirit.

And there is that cow, as well!

July, 1995

How to Tell Renata

Linda Holeman

fact (fakt) n. something that has
actually occurred or actually exists.

It's rained the entire summer, and the air is heavy with the smell of an old basement.

The rain and the smell and the worrying about how to tell Renata what's happening are driving me crazy, and I've hardly been able to put the dictionary down. I know there's some old joke about reading the phone book. I can't remember it, but it's not flattering. I tell myself that a dictionary is nothing like a phone book, except that it's in alphabetical order. This is the very thing I find calming — the predictability of the next word. I've been reading the dictionary my whole life, it seems, although sometimes I can forget about it for a while. But for the last few months I've really needed it.

Our summers are known for their unrelenting prairie heat, so this cool, wet one is a real change. Not knowing how to talk to Renata is nothing new.

Renata is my mother — though I've never called her anything but Renata for as long as I can remember — and this is the way she's always dealt with things. By ignoring them. Maybe it's because she's been on her own, except for me, pretty much all of her life, and there was never anyone else for her to talk to.

But even now that she's had Jerry around for almost two years, things still haven't changed much with the way we try to communicate.

Renata's okay, as far as small things go, but keeps quiet on anything large and frightening. This is how I see it — she must think if the scary stuff is pushed to some far, webby corner of her cranium, shrouded and silent, then perhaps it doesn't really exist, and can't be turned into a fact.

Maybe it works sometimes; after all, what's scaring me hasn't become an actual fact.

But it's only a matter of time.

> *Chimera* (ka mir a) n. An absurd
> creation of the imagination; a foolish
> or horrible fancy.

School starts in eight days. I know I should be getting out my supply list, should go and try to find my gym clothes at the bottom of my closet, should get my hair trimmed, should do all those back-to-school things that some people say they enjoy. But I can't seem to get motivated; like I said, all I've been doing is the dictionary thing.

The most interesting word I found last night was *chimera*. I had a rush of hope; maybe what seems to be happening is all a chimera, just the old imagination working overtime.

I held on to the word, whispering it over and over as I tried to fall asleep after Renata had left for her shift at the Muffins Day 'N Night over on Provencher. I kept my eyes fixed on the lamp beside my bed, the pink glow through the faded shade. I leave it on now, the nights Renata works.

As I chanted it, my word took on the pulse of a prayer, the syllables moving in rhythm with this summer's night sounds — the rising and falling murmur of the television in the living room, the slow ticking of the rain off the eaves outside my window, and the stealthy rush, then triumphant clang as the trains coupled in the yards across the river.

And even though there wasn't any air coming in through the screen, just that musty, underground smell, I kept the blankets wrapped around me, and I held on to my word for all the comfort I could wring out of it.

> *Realization* (re el i za shen) n. The conversion into fact or action of plans, ambitions, fears, etc.

The problem is that Renata loves Jerry. When he moved in, she had seemed all sparkly, and almost pretty. I think it was the first time I'd seen her totally happy. For a whole year, Jerry remembered all the important times, like her birthday and Valentine's Day, and he took her out for dinner, twice a month, on payday.

I'm not exactly sure when things started to go bad, but I remember feeling weird one night, when Renata was at work and Jerry and I were watching some National Geographic show about whales. I was really into the show, when it slowly dawned on me that Jerry was looking at me, and not the television. But when I turned toward him his eyes flicked back to the screen. The next time I felt his eyes on me I got up and went to my room.

He did it a lot, after that first time. Watched me, but pretended he wasn't. It didn't seem like such a big deal. I didn't like it, but I could live with it.

Then one evening, some time around the beginning of the summer, I was cutting a tomato at the counter. He walked up behind me and put his hand on the back of my neck. I kept on cutting, hoping he'd go away, but he just stood there, his hand still and warm, getting heavier with each second. When the tomato was all sliced I put the knife down, and he gave my neck a squeeze, just a little one, and then slowly moved his hand down my back.

After he left I noticed I'd sliced into my finger with the paring knife, and it was bleeding everywhere, but the strange thing was it didn't hurt until a lot later.

Since then I feel like my life has become this big bubble, and I'm walking around inside it, trying not to break through. It's hard to concentrate on anything. I feel like I can't hear properly; the bubble is causing pressure in my ears so I have to keep swallowing and swallowing to clear them.

Not being able to hear makes it hard for words to come too. No matter how I rehearse what I'll say to Renata, it sounds wrong in my own head.

I guess I figure that either way it's going to kill her, and we'll both lose. If she doesn't believe me, she'll hate me, thinking I'm lying about the guy she loves. Or maybe she will believe me, and hate me even more.

> *Ripe* (rip) adj. Grown to maturity,
> fully developed. 2. In full readiness
> to do or try; prepared.

I knew, after waking up sometime in the middle of the night to see Jerry standing in my doorway again, that I couldn't count on chimera. I knew that time was running out — knew with that same awful certainty that you know the dull throbbing in your back molar is a cavity you'll have to get filled.

Lying in bed in the thin grey morning light, understanding that today was the day I had to do it, I was overwhelmed with a sensation of heavy lightness, or maybe it was light heaviness. Relief, mixed with terror. Sort of like deciding that today is the day you'll finally jump off the high diving board at the community swimming pool.

It was late in the afternoon before I had a chance. I came into the kitchen after I finished work, my summer job at the California Fruit Market. I'm not officially old enough for a job, not until I turn sixteen next year, but my friend Lindsay MacJannet's father owns the market. She got her dad to pay us cash to do odd jobs around the place. We'd unpack the boxes, pick over berries for mushy ones, check the apples for bruises, those kinds of things.

As I came into the kitchen I shifted my watermelon from arm to arm. It was a dense, tubular, dark green melon, a gift from Mr. MacJannet. He gave me whatever was too ripe to wait any longer. Between my soft strawberries and speckled bananas, and the two-day-old stuff Renata could bring home from Muffins Day 'N Night, we'd covered at least two of the food groups at no expense all summer.

Renata was sitting at the kitchen table. She was in her uniform, a pink, short-sleeved dress that buttoned up the front, the skirt of the dress covered by a white apron. She was pushing back her cuticles with a small pointed stick. I could hear the television, so I knew Jerry was in the living room.

"What's going on?" I don't know what made me ask; Renata working on her nails and Jerry watching TV is a totally normal scene in our house. But there was something else, something I couldn't quite catch, like I just missed the last few words in a whispered conversation, or someone quietly slipped out the back door.

Renata didn't answer, or even look up at me. I set the watermelon on the counter with a dull thud, then sat down on the scratched wooden chair beside Renata and watched her.

"School starts in less than a week," I said to Renata's bent, blonde head, noticing that there was half an inch of darker hair, light brown mixed with coarse threads of silver, along her part. I didn't really expect a response, but after a minute she looked up, right into my eyes.

"So soon?" she asked, and put down her stick.

I nodded, and the way her eyes held on to mine brought a sudden, hopeful surge of blood into my throat.

"So, are you ready?" she asked. "Are you scared, about starting high school?"

"Not really," I said, not caring which question she thought I was answering, and then, "Mom?" It was weird, how it just came out. Like I said, I've always called her Renata. As soon as I said the word, *Mom*, I saw her pupils get big, then immediately shrink, like a match had been lit in front of them. She lowered her eyes, picking up the stick again, but just studied the pointed end, holding it out in front of her like a tiny sword. I wanted to say it again, *Mom*; it had felt good on my tongue and lips, but I didn't want to push it. Instead, I reached out and pressed the pad of my index finger against the point of the stick.

"Renata? I need to talk to you. There's something I need your help with."

Renata kept looking at the stick, and I looked at it, too. It was creating a minuscule hole in the soft flesh of my finger as I pressed harder and harder. The stick joined our hands on the smooth, brown arborite of the table top, and as I stared at it, felt the far-off flutter of a wing. Black, its weight shutting off my air supply. I took short, furtive sniffs through my nose, afraid that even those would break the spell, not let me say what I had to.

Suddenly Renata's head jerked up, from my hand to a spot over my head. I turned. Jerry was in the doorway. He was good at that, appearing in doorways.

Without taking her eyes off Jerry, Renata said, "Well, Jacinda, I need some help, too. With supper. If I don't get a start on it I'll be late for my shift." She sort of hoisted herself out of the chair, even though she's really thin, and then slowly walked to the sink.

Jerry followed her. He put his hand on the watermelon, then looked at me.

"Should we have this for dessert?" he asked.

I shrugged, looking at Renata, standing still and straight, her hands flat on the counter on either side of the sink. I saw that her pink dress was creased across the seat, and the ends of her apron were tied at the small of her back in a loose, lop-sided bow. Even without lifting my eyes from the bow, I could tell that Renata had turned her head and was staring at Jerry again. I kept my gaze on the bow, and took a slow, deep breath.

I had gone to the edge of the diving board and was looking over. There was no room to turn around.

> *Illuminate* (i loo me nat) v. 1. To give
> light to; light up. 2. To shed light
> upon; clarify. 3. To enlighten, as the
> mind.

Supper had the flavour and consistency of cardboard; all the swallowing was affecting my taste buds, too.

"Pass the butter, please," I said to Renata. As she handed it to me, I asked, as casually as I could, "How much longer will you be on nights?" I set the butter dish down and pressed the tip of my knife into the soft yellow rectangle.

"For at least another three weeks," Renata said. "But they're changing my shift on Monday. Instead of eight to four I have to move to the later shift, midnight to eight."

I made a sound that could have meant anything. What I was thinking was that I would tell her when she got home from work, even if it was 4:30 in the morning.

And that I wouldn't stay in this house without her one more night.

* * *

After I was done the dishes I wrote a note, *Went to stay overnight with Lindsay,* and propped it against the toaster. I didn't want Jerry to start looking for me and call Renata. Grabbing my jacket, I slipped out the back door. I wanted to avoid going past the living room, where the television was transmitting its sad blue light.

I took a bus downtown and went to the Salisbury House on Garry Street, the one that stays open until one o'clock. I sat there with a plate of fries until closing time, then started walking home. I knew it would take over two hours, giving me less than an hour and a half to wait for Renata. I planned to sit out in the backyard on a lawn chair, so I could see the car lights as she pulled into the driveway. Then I could catch her before she went into the house, sit down on the front step and tell her, without any interruptions.

Every time I thought of the words rolling out of my mouth, and what her face would look like, I got this thick greasy feeling in my stomach, even though I hadn't even eaten any of the fries. The greasiness kept threatening to push its way up my throat.

To take my mind off feeling sick, I concentrated on walking, thinking of nothing else except the pressure of the rubber soles of my sneakers on the pavement. But after a while I couldn't help but notice that there was a mist rolling around me, and my left heel had a burning blister. I started to count off the streets before mine. One block away the mist turned to fine drops, and within five minutes it was a regular downpour, and I was soaked.

I looked at my watch. Only 2:45; I was ahead of schedule, and waiting in the rain wasn't appealing. But as I walked up our street, I could see that Renata's car was in the driveway. The fins of the old Chrysler Renata had driven since I was a baby stuck up over the low hedge around our yard like some ancient, displaced shark.

Renata never left work early.

As I reached out to put my key in the lock, I saw that the front door wasn't even closed all the way. I gave it a tiny push, and it swung open.

I stepped through and closed it silently behind me. The house was in darkness except for one soft light, spilling into the hall from Renata and Jerry's bedroom. I took off my dripping jacket and dropped it on the mat, then moved down the hall as noiselessly as I could.

Renata was at her window, looking out through the black square. In the light from the lamp on the dresser I could see her reflection, but the rain drops rolling down the glass changed her features. They were blended into one another, creating a softer, smoothed out Renata, except for her mouth. It was still in its stitched, straight line. Her arms were crossed against the pink material of her chest.

I could see my own reflection, too, the distance and light and wet glass distorting my image so I looked like a bigger version of myself, filling the doorway.

I listened to the silence of the house, closing my eyes. When I opened them and looked around the room I noticed that the closet door was open, and something was different, but I wasn't sure what it was.

My eyes moved from the empty hangers back to Renata's reflection, and when I took my first step into the room, I saw her shoulders flinch, and I knew that she could see my image, there in the window. As I watched, the stitches that held her mouth started to loosen, unravel the tiniest bit.

And as I walked toward her, my sneakers moving faster and faster, making tiny, damp, mewing sounds on the bare wood floor, I saw my mother's arms unfold from across her chest and rise, opening, as if caught in an unexpected, upward current of air.

Bulat Kisses

Jacqueline Pinto

The sky was still dark as she lay in bed, gazing at the folds of blue netting draped around her. She listened to the crows scraping the air with their screams and the geckoes chirping their last good mornings before twisting back into the eaves. Throwing her legs over the side of the mattress, she bent forward and pulled herself up slowly, holding her head back to let the blue lace border brush deliciously along her face: from her chin to her lips and nose and over her forehead and hair. She imagined fingers drawing a veil from her face and a soft palm against her cheek. Spinning around the room in her nightdress, she landed in front of the mirror. Squealing, she bent forward with a kiss to the glass. As she gazed at herself her smile cracked and fell. Frowning, she picked a strand of lizard dung from her hair. She pressed her head with her fingertips and glared at the mosquito net, then grabbed her toothbrush and headed for the well.

* * *

Sujata pulled at the rope, hefting a bucket of water from the mossy depths of the well. Her sister sat in a corner, poking her toes in the sand. "Nelum," she said as she poured the water into a small, plastic basin, "what are you doing here?"

"Why should I tell you?" said Nelum.

Sujata began brushing her teeth. "Because I asked."

Nelum snorted and lifted her skirt.

"Hey!" Toothpaste dripped from Sujata's chin. Nelum squatted next to her sister's feet and grinned, baring her knees. "Nelum!"

"You think I'm going to piss?" Nelum leered at her sister. Sujata backed away, toothbrush wedged in her mouth. Nelum flared her nostrils. "What do you think I am?" Sujata looked away. When she turned back again, Nelum had disappeared, leaving a steaming hole in the sand.

As she entered the kitchen, Sujata was comforted by the mingling scents of burning wood and fried onions. "Good morning, *Siya*,"* she said to the old man at the table.

"Good morning, *duwa*."* Sujata sat across from her grandfather and reached for a mound of *kiri bat*.* From the corner of her eye she watched his hands, now sun-black, wrinkled, with chipped nails. The long fingers dug into a hill of milk rice, extracted a portion and rolled it around into two tight balls. These he set aside on the edge of his plate before beginning to eat his breakfast.

"*Siya*, who will I meet today?"

The old man looked at his daughter and smiled. "A nice one."

"What will we do?"

"Talk."

Sujata studied three ants scurrying towards the plantains near her plate. "And if I don't like him?"

"Then you don't like him."

"I don't usually like them."

The old man gave her a long look. "*Duwa*, stop this talk and eat."

Siya: grandfather
duwa: daughter
kiri bat: rice made with coconut milk

Sujata opened, then closed her mouth. She pushed some rice and *pol sambol** between her lips and chewed. She watched the old man as he peeled a sour plantain, carefully laying its limp yellow petals on the table.

Siya rose from his chair, plate in hand, and she followed him as he stepped outside. From behind an aloe plant she saw her grandfather holding his right hand, palm open, to the sky; two rice balls sat in the cushion of his hand. A breeze blew and the trees began to dance. The aloe furled and unfurled itself. The sky darkened as thick clouds closed around the sun. Leaves whipped the air and Sujata's face. Through the splaying coconut palms came a loud flapping of wings and a flurry of blue and black feathers. In the whirl of beating wings, Sujata saw a patch of white hair, the edge of a smile, a piece of cheek. Then everything: her grandfather in turquoise sarong and white undershirt, right hand held high, and the yellow sun streaming between empty fingers.

* * *

"*Aacchi,** which one do you think is better, the red or the blue?" Sujata held the corners of two saris, one in each hand. "I prefer the blue."

"Then blue it shall be." Sujata's grandmother showed a chipped, coffee-stained smile. "*Duwa,* get me some *bulat.*"* Sujata dropped the silks and bent to a short, pedestaled tray laden with green, heart-shaped betel leaves. Her grandmother pulled out what looked like an old silver watch-case, opened it, and scraped out some *chunam.** Her short fingers darted between a miniature brass mortar and piles of ingredients:

---

pol sambol: spicy shredded coconut
aacchi: grandmother, old woman
bulat: a mixture of tobacco, arecanut, and lime wrapped in a betel leaf and chewed; mild intoxicant
chunam: a sticky white substance obtained from roasting chalk

tobacco, arecanut, and betel. Swiftly she plucked the decora-
tive pestle from her necklace and pounded for almost a
minute before pinching a wad and popping it into her mouth.
The old woman then sat back in her chair, relaxing her jaws
into a steady chewing rhythm. "You . . . mm . . . said *de . . .
luwa*, what were you say . . ."

Sujata picked up the two sari ends again.

"Ah . . . mm. Yes. Blue aw led."

Sujata gazed at the rolling lump in her *Aacchi*'s cheek.
"Blue."

"Yes . . . mm. Glue." *Aacchi* squeezed the cud against the
roof of her mouth. Red foamed at the corners of her lips.
"*Dluwa*, you must dress nicely today. Don't forget your gold
chains and bangles. And your hair," she stretched her fingers
out to her granddaughter's head, "we must oil your hair well."

Sujata cringed. "Oil? Do we have to?"

Aacchi sucked her cheek. "Yes, now come, let's do a wash."

Sujata's shoulders drooped. "Yes, *Aacchi*."

They walked outside. "*Duwa*," *Aacchi* stroked the girl's hair,
"today is a very important day. The boy is from a rich home
— the father is a doctor. A doctor, child, do you understand?"
Sujata nodded. "Good." The old woman turned her head and
spat, leaving a bright red arc in the sand.

Sujata returned to the kitchen and found Nelum standing
by the oven. Sujata smiled. "What?" said Nelum, leaning
against the concrete. Behind her, clay pots perched on bricks
amidst leaping flames. Smoke spiralled around Nelum's hair.

"Are you cooking?"

"Why should I?"

"Not *should* you, are you?"

"Leave me alone." Nelum turned to a counter heaped with
red onions. Slowly she picked one up and began skinning it
with her fingernails, then tossed it into a basket. Before the

naked onion landed, Nelum had already peeled another. The papery skins peppered up into the air, and a small cyclone of black flies whirled over the detritus. Nelum's hands moved quickly, working themselves into a blur of purplish-red, white, and brown. Sujata watched with raised brows and slightly tearing eyes.

"Do you need some help?" she offered timidly. Nelum, deaf to the sounds around her, continued the tedious business, eyes dry and wide with concentration.

Sujata wandered towards her bedroom, remembering the stories her mother had told her about her older sister. She saw, with a strange clarity, the servant woman playing with a month-old Nelum, throwing her up into the air and catching her, up into the air and catching her again. The child shrieked with delight, punching the air with tiny fists and feet, shaking in her diaper as she flew and hicupping when she landed in the servant's strong hands. Howling gleefully, she was thrust into the air again, her excited kicks becoming more vigorous as she descended. Down, down she came. The servant stretched out her arms. But Nelum kept falling, falling and laughing until her head hit the cement floor.

"We sacked the stupid woman, of course," Sujata's mother had said, "but what was the use in the end?" Sujata juggled the myths in her memory. Balloons filled with strange helium visions squeezed from her ears into the midmorning heat. She saw her eldest brother hugging a thirteen-year-old Nelum to his chest, trying to carry her to the outhouse while the girl's feet dragged stubbornly along the ground. "Leave me alone," she had barked, spitting at her brother when he found her squatting on the staircase outside the house. "I'm not going into that stinking shit-house."

And she saw an older Nelum at the well, bath sarong
forming a puddle at her ankles, village boys crowding behind
bushes, pointing and laughing.

"Get out!" screamed Nelum as she pelted the jeering
children with stones. "Get out, you dirty bastards!" But the
boys, granted the sight of Nelum's swaying wet breasts, let out
a rapturous sigh and winked at one another, swooning in the
ecstasy of a July afternoon.

* * *

" . . . found your sarong yet, child?" Sujata felt the tail end
of her grandmother's words licking the back of her neck.
Tripping into her room, she yanked a thin green cloth off her
chair. Quickly she pulled off her dress, wrapped the cloth
around her chest, and ran down the hallway through the
kitchen to the well.

"What were you doing all this time? We don't have time for
games, child."

Sujata blinked at the red drops which spattered her cheeks
and brow. "Nothing."

"*Ayo,** duwa*, he is a very nice boy from an important family.
Don't you remember what I told you? You must impress him."

"But what if I don't like him?"

Aacchi stared at Sujata with wide eyes. "Don't like? Don't
like?" A scarlet stream gushed from the old woman's withering
lips. "Nonsense!" She drew the spittle back into her mouth.
"If he likes you, that's all that matters."

"But *Siya* said — "

"Never mind what *Siya* said."

"But — "

---

ayo: an exclamation equivalent to "oh!"

"Hold your head down."

"But — "

"Hold your head down."

"But — "

Aacchi grabbed Sujata's head and pushed it down, then dumped a pale of cold water on it. Sujata squirmed.

"Keep your head like that." The old woman continued to empty bucket after bucket onto Sujata's shivering body. Sujata felt her sarong sticking to her thighs and breasts. Her skin broke out in goose pimples.

"Take this soap."

Sujata carefully lathered herself beneath the cloth, rinsing immediately afterward. Again she submitted to her bucket-brandishing *Aacchi*. Another stream of cold water slapped her shoulders, and Sujata clutched at her sarong.

When it was over, Sujata stood, skin smarting from the cold water, sarong dripping over her hips and breasts, hair steaming in the hot sun. She squinted at the brightness of the sky and the plumpness of the clouds, and soon began to relish the midday heat which massaged her spine and buttocks. She turned and lifted her arms to the blue ocean above her, hugging the warmth which cascaded over her chest and stomach. Stretching further, she inhaled the hypnotic light, kissing its fingers. And slowly, as her back arched toward the yellow fire, her sarong slipped from her breast. Sujata, entranced by the heat stirring inside her, closed her eyes and tasted the fragrant breath of the sun.

"Sujata! Sujata!"

Flaming arrows pierced her navel. Eyes still shut, she saw orange birds of paradise flapping wings of fire, stretching golden claws towards her heart.

"What is this, child, are you mad?" Sujata was caught in a swarm of burning feathers; flaming tongues licked her back and calves. "Child!" She took deep, rapturous breaths, but the heat began to blister her skin.

"*Sujata.*" The heat became more intense. Plumes of fire receded. Sujata opened her eyes and blinked away tears. She felt a stinging slap on her back and turned around to see her grandmother, palm raised and angled towards her. She jumped away and realized for the first time that she was completely naked.

"*Buddhu ammo!*"* cried *Aacchi.* Sujata grabbed the green sarong and quickly wrapped it around her. "*Oyate pissu!* Mad, you're mad!"

Sujata bit her lip. "It fell," she said, rubbing her eye, "I guess I didn't . . . " her ears began to burn, "I mean, I didn't . . ."

"Shut up." *Aacchi* bared her brown-stained teeth. "You were standing shamelessly like a . . . like a . . . " She stopped and pounded her chest. "Nelum, get me some *bulat.*"

Sujata fled towards her room, knocking Nelum aside as she passed through the kitchen. "Can't anyone get any work done here without interruption?" Nelum's annoyed, onion-dipped words slammed through Sujata's ears, but she kept running until she reached the sanctuary of her room.

She paced in front of her bed. "This is all wrong," she said to the almirah. "If he likes you, that's all that matters. If he likes you, that's all that matters." The words spilled onto the polished red floor. Sujata stepped on them.

"Nelum, have you seen the oil anywhere?" It was *Aacchi* coming down the corridor. Sujata froze for a moment, then towelled her hair and body, leapt into a dress and slipped out the window. Within the sixty seconds it took for her

---

buddhu ammo: an expression meaning "mother of the Buddha", equivalent to "oh my God!"

grandmother to locate the oil and turn the knob of the bedroom door, Sujata made it to the freedom of the red clay road.

* * *

Barefoot, she walked along the gravel, sheltered from the sun by looming jack and mango trees. Crotons, with warped yellow and green leaves, rustled in the breeze. Bright red and pink anthuriums nodded heart-shaped heads at her knees. Coconut trees leaned into a solid blue sky. Sujata giggled and reached into her dress pocket. From its yellow cotton depths she pulled out a rolled up betel leaf. She pressed it between her fingers, squeezing the lime and arecanut inside. Then folding it into a rough square, she put it into her mouth and began chewing. She could feel it spraying between her teeth, and pursed her lips against the rising, red tide. Crimson squirted from the left corner of her mouth. Sujata spat to release pressure, then resumed chewing.

As she gazed at bulbous jack fruits weighing toward the ground, her head began to feel lighter and lighter. She walked and the road rippled beneath her feet. A dog strayed in front of her, squatting to release a steaming swirl of green. Sujata shifted her focus to the peacock fan of a distant talipot palm. It swayed left and right with the wind, languidly fanning the clouds. And Sujata tipped from side to side in imitation, gently tossing her hair in the rising heat.

Stepping into a sun-drenched stretch of road, Sujata felt her eyes swelling from the fierceness of the noonday sun. She blinked at the surrounding paddy fields extending deep into the horizon. On her left, a lone crane stood white hot against a blue and green background. A herd of water buffalo, elephant grey, ambled into the water on her right, nosing the reeds and shaking their coiled horns.

She marvelled at their glistening muscles and remembered: *ghostly faces rising out of darkness and dust, horns curling toward her. The earth shudders and a man, thin with terrifying white eyes, cries out from the midst of a buffalo maëlstrom. "He can't see," screams a voice and Sujata jumps to the side of a trembling road. Eyes closed, she listens to bellowing hooves, slapping skin, and the "Hup! Hup! Hup!" of the blind buffalo driver.* Her ears fill with the sound of a piercing wind. It sucks her organs and shakes her ribs and Sujata, palms pressed against her ears, realizes that she is screaming.

Sujata wiped the sweat from her upper lip with her hand. She continued to watch the water buffalo, now circling in the field. Their grey bodies lumbered through the water, jolting Sujata's already muddled thoughts. At the centre, a black piece of wood bobbed up and down with a strange rhythm. Sujata squinted, thinking that the wood seemed somehow familiar. She bent closer, rubbing her forehead.

"Nelum?" The piece of wood twisted oddly.

"Nelum! *Akka!*"* Sujata jumped into the water and began wading toward her sister. "Are you crazy? They'll kill you."

Nelum swam between two buffalo as though they were trees. "*Aacchi* is looking for you, she wants to oil your head."

Sujata watched with a deep frown as Nelum climbed the bank. Her mouth fell open. "Nelum, where's your underwear?"

"Underwear? Are you mad? Do you want me to wear more layers of clothing in this bloody heat?"

Sujata stared at the brown moon of Nelum's behind, poking prominently through the faded print of her cotton dress. "But Nelum, you . . . you can't . . . "

---

akka: older sister; *akké* is the vocative of the same word

"Just shut up and go home."

"Please." Sujata saw two men approaching on bicycles. "Please Nelum, let's both go . . . "

"No. *You* go. I am *not* going to pound any more *bulat* for that soggy old bitch."

"Ané, * akké."*

"Go."

Sujata sighed and shook her head. She spat out the last of the betel from her mouth and began a slow walk home. "Piss off!" She heard in the distance, and turned around to see her sister throwing rocks at the two cyclists.

* * *

Sujata approached the house from the side. Back pressed against the wall, she slid toward her room, tiptoeing along the concrete edge of the gutters. Seeing that the room was empty, she crept through the window, and on hands and knees, crawled across the floor to shut the door. Standing in the middle of the room, she stripped off her damp dress and stepped into a thin underskirt. Quickly she hooked up the front of her purple jacket, and wound a blue paisley sari around her hips. She chose two gold bangles for her left wrist, and around her neck she placed a simple gold chain. Voices echoed down the corridor from the front hall.

"He's here," cried *Aacchi.*

"But where is Sujata?" *Siya* sounded worried.

Sujata looked at herself in the mirror. She puckered her lips, now bright red from the betel, and winked. "I'm here, *Siya.* I'm coming."

---

ané. a pleading expression

Sujata allowed herself to be led by her grandmother down the hallway to the veranda.

"Where have you been?" the old lady whispered crossly into the girl's ear. "We've been looking everywhere for you. And look at your hair — you didn't even oil it."

Sujata rolled her eyes.

Six cane chairs were placed around a small table on the veranda. One chair was occupied by a young man with thin hair and plain brown eyes. On either side of him sat a plump man and woman.

"Sujata," *Aacchi* held her granddaughter's elbow, "this is Dr. and Mrs. Premaratne and their son, Sreeja." She pointed at the chair directly in front of the boy. "You can sit there." Sujata smiled, careful not to show her teeth. The boy smiled back. *Aacchi* and *Siya* took seats on either side of their granddaughter.

"How is Mrs. Abeysekere?" began Dr. Premaratne.

"My daughter," said *Siya*, "is still in the hospital. She has been having kidney trouble."

Sujata started at the mention of her mother.

"I'm sorry to hear of it," continued Dr. Premaratne. "And Mr. Abeysekere? I understand he is away on business."

"Yes," *Siya* gritted his teeth, "on business . . . in Nuwera Eliya."

Sujata winced, remembering that the racing season had just begun. Before he had left for Nuwera Eliya, Sujata's father had promised to bet on a horse for his daughter. She cried as he slipped her ruby earrings into his pocket. "I'll bring back even bigger ones," he had said, and kissed her on the forehead.

"Sujata has just completed her O-levels," *Aacchi* quickly veered the conversation toward her granddaughter.

Sujata bowed her head.

"Oh," said Sreeja, "and what subjects do you prefer?"

"History."

"And?"

"Literature."

"I was never very interested in those areas myself, but then, those are good subjects for young ladies."

Sujata's eyes narrowed. "And what do you enjoy?"

"Mathematics and, of course, physics."

"Very manly subjects indeed . . . "

Sreeja beamed.

" . . . but do you do well in them?"

Sreeja shifted in his chair. "I do well enough, I think."

Sujata glared at her toes, lips pursed.

Sreeja smiled at the young lady before him. Her thick black braids and dark eyes amazed him. And the defiant blush of her lips made his palms sweat. He wiped his hands on his thighs. "Sujata," he whispered softly to his knees.

"Yes?"

"What?" Sreeja looked shocked. "Uh . . . some water, I'd like some water, please."

Sujata watched as *Aacchi* poured a glass for Sreeja. She looked at the boy's limp, brownish hair, his light brown eyes, and skin the colour of milky tea. A sneer tripped across her upper lip. Out of the corner of her eye, Sujata glanced at *Siya*. His furrowed cheeks and arms like polished ebony comforted her. She turned back to Sreeja, whose Adam's apple bobbed and rolled with the waves of water he pushed down his throat.

Sreeja, feeling Sujata's stare piercing his neck, poured himself another glass of water. The redness of her lips was driving him mad, and the hardness of her eyes sparked a fire in the pit of his stomach.

Sujata and Sreeja stared over one another's heads. *Aacchi*, disturbed by the silence, pinched her granddaughter and turned to Sreeja's mother. "Mrs. Premaratne," she said, "you must be very proud of your son."

"Yes," said Dr. Premaratne as his wife opened her mouth to speak, "in a few years, he will be an engineer. We intend to send him to England or Australia."

Siya raised his brows. "England or Australia? When?"

"In a few years. There's time."

Mrs. Premaratne nodded. "There's time," she said.

Sujata gazed at the distant coconut trees, drooping like huge dandelions, up toward the sky. She watched the sun, a blood orange, staining the horizon salmon pink, and remembered the mystery of that morning: her grandfather's offering, the congested sky, the tremendous wings of an unknown bird. For a moment she felt the ecstatic heat of the midday sun against her chest. She thought she saw fingers, receding into the sky, but it was only Nelum.

Sujata sat up abruptly in her chair. *Aacchi*, turning in the direction of Sujata's gaze, stiffened. Nelum strolled up to the veranda. Her body, lit up by a brilliant sunset, shone through her wet dress. Mr. and Mrs. Premaratne dropped their jaws in unison. Sreeja, stunned by the sight of Nelum's breasts pointing between the blue flowers of her dress, crossed his legs. He looked furtively at his lap, then turned guiltily to face Sujata. But Sujata could only smile at her sister.

"What is everyone looking at? Take your dirty eyes off my body." Nelum stalked into the house. "Goddamn idiots," she muttered, "why don't they keep their eyes on their own tits."

Sujata grinned.

Sreeja's eyes widened. As those beautiful lips parted, Sreeja wilted. He grimaced at the stains wedged between Sujata's teeth. His stomach turned at the sight of red saliva, like elastics of coagulated blood, hanging from her gums. Kali, he thought, it is the demon Kali sitting before me, grinding flesh

between her razor-like teeth. Her eyes bulged and in their
blackness he saw himself falling onto the cushion of her
serpentine tongue, sliding under the pounding ivory of her
dreadful molars. Sreeja leaned back in his chair, desperately
trying to avoid being sucked into the gaping jaws. He closed
his eyes, shutting out the bloody lips. And as he pushed his
chair backward to distance himself from the beast, the cane
legs slipped away and he fell in a faint to the floor.

* * *

Sujata lay in bed, listening to the grunting frogs and squeaking lizards. The moon cast a shaft of silver light across the red
floor. She rubbed her cheek which still stung from *Aacchi's*
slaps. "Who told you to take my *bulat?*" she had yelled between
beatings. *"Val ganni,* you dirty woman. *Oomba harima modai . . .*
foolish, foolish child." *Siya* hadn't said a word. He only sighed
and stared at the clouds.

That evening, Sujata had stood in the hall by the kitchen,
silently listening to the words of a crooked man with one long
pink thumbnail. "It's no use, *mahattaya*"* he had said to *Siya,*
"it's written in the stars. She won't marry until she is thirty or
thirty-one years old."

Sujata smiled to herself, wiping the salt stains from either
side of her nose. She looked up toward the ceiling. The
mosquito net, knotted above the bed, was a powder blue
hot-air balloon floating through an ocean of moonlight.

---

mahattaya: respectful address meaning "sir"

My War

Budge Wilson

"I love the war." My lips formed the words, but there was no sound. Although young, I knew that it was an indecent thing to love the war. I was not entirely stupid. I knew that fathers and brothers died, and occasionally sisters. Newspapers and the radio brought news every day of ships sinking, cities being bombed, widows weeping, children bereft. It was unthinkable to love the war, and there I was, doing it. So I felt guilty; I told no one; but I allowed myself the luxury of my own private feelings. The time was 1941, during some of the darkest days of the Second World War. The place was Halifax, in Nova Scotia. I was fourteen years old.

Later, I was to realize that the First and Second World Wars were not, after all, so very far apart. My own father had returned from the first one, just twenty-one years before the second one began. I now know that twenty-one years is a very short time. When I was fourteen, it seemed like an endless stretch of years. It was history. It was the past. And the past was not attractive to me unless it could be made to seem vivid, dramatic. Thus, it mystified and infuriated me that my father refused to talk about his own war. Why? I wanted to hear colourful tales of brave deeds on the battlefields, long heroic marches over treacherous terrain, the mournful sounds of the Last Post, stoicism in the face of extreme pain.

"Tell me about it," I'd beg. "Describe to me what it was like. *Please*, Dad."

But he would tell me nothing. His face would take on what I came to call his "war mask", and he'd say, "Sorry, Lisa. I'm just not ready to talk about it."

Ready! If he wasn't ready after twenty-one years, what were the possibilities of his *ever* being ready? When I watched him listening to the news on the day that war was declared in 1939, I think I knew that day would never come. When he rose from his chair to leave the room (the warm September sun streaming through the window, lighting up the pots of blazing geraniums on the sill) — his face bleak, his shoulders slumped — I could see that he was crying.

What a surprise, then, to find so much to enjoy in this new war. The streets of Halifax — damp and grey for so long — were suddenly alive with laughing sailors, jaunty in their bell-bottom trousers and cocky hats. With my best friend, Daisy, I cruised through the busy sidewalks of the downtown, agape at the spectacle. We listened to the energetic voices of the WRENS, who swung along Barrington Street in their snappy outfits, conscious of new roles for themselves, new power; our eager adolescent eyes feasted on the handsome men lounging on the stone walls of the Grand Parade, sporting uniforms from countries I'd scarcely heard of. The waters of Bedford Basin were constantly crammed with scores of ships, awaiting departure for mysterious and dangerous places. And the silent, secret convoys, slipping out of the Basin and along the harbour, never failed to move me. Daisy and I pored over pictures of ships struggling through heavy waves on winter seas, superstructures layered with ice, men clinging to the handrails, their faces grim.

How I longed to be on one of those ships, bound for adventures that I was sure I could easily cope with. I pictured myself limping bravely through foreign streets, strewn with the debris left behind by bombs: broken glass; piles of bricks and powdered plaster; barefaced buildings open like dolls' houses, whole walls torn away; people bent over, searching through the rubble for lost belongings. But I was fine. In spite of my limp (some sort of wound was always featured in these scenes), ignoring my gnawing hunger, I was marching ahead with purpose and strength. A nurse? (Carrying my black bag, on my way to the overcrowded hospital, its corridors loud with cries of torment.) A spy? (Lurking in dark alleyways, clutching my case of coded documents, sliding along with my back to the wall, alert, *ready*.) A member of the Canadian Women's Army Corps? (Erect, neglecting my injuries, my uniform torn and marked by splinters and dirt — and blood? — nonetheless complementing my excellent figure.) I didn't have an excellent figure in 1941, but inaccuracies never impeded the forward movement of my dreams, by day or by night. And no suffering presented itself that I was unable to bear, no task too difficult or too dangerous.

Real life in Halifax could be almost as dramatic as my fantasies. I revelled in the black nights, made dark by thousands of sets of blackout curtains. I was thrilled by the searchlights practising in the sky, chasing the tiny silver planes, catching them, losing them, sweeping across the night sky with their giant fingers. I took pleasure in the crowded streets; the reeling drunks, laughing, singing; the sight of the drab old city, dressed up, brought alive — yet again — by a global conflict. Yes. I loved the war.

In other ways, life continued on, much as before. Basically, I guess I was fond of my family, but they all irritated me with varying degrees of intensity. My father, shell-shocked in the First World War, had a remoteness about him that was difficult to penetrate, and I resented this. My mother was sensitive and loving, but far too concerned about my safety and happiness. My brother, Jeremy, was a full-fledged ten-year-old pest —

showing off, teasing me, tormenting the cat, eating more than his share of everything. But then there was Daisy.

Daisy called for me each weekday morning, and we walked to school, talking and talking — discussing the teachers' various peculiarities, picking flaws in our friends, condemning the intricacies of mathematics. In late afternoon, we did our homework together at alternate houses. Afterward, on the telephone, we described the servicemen and women who had come to our houses for last Sunday's dinner. We complained about the absurd restrictions set up by our parents. (My mother, for example, forbade me to walk in Point Pleasant Park, the 186 acres of woods in the south of Halifax, unless accompanied by an adult — all this, in spite of my impatient assurances to her that I was exceptionally strong and could easily fend off any attacker.) We discussed, with admiration, jealousy, and scorn, the peculiarities of the English Guest Children who attended our school, safe from the bombs, but not from the hazards of Canadian peer pressure and incompatible foster homes.

Daisy and I also talked about boys, sex, and the future possibilities of love. In spite of the surrounding hordes of handsome servicemen, both of us were deeply in love with Mr. Grant, our new history teacher. He was rumoured to be exceptionally fond of his dark-haired wife, and he also had a small daughter of whom he was said to be extravagantly proud. None of this prevented us from creating elaborate daydreams centred around his secret attraction to me or to Daisy. In spite of a severe football injury which had kept him out of the war, he was built like an Olympic athlete — tall, strong, young. He was a teacher, but also a listener (rare, we felt, among teachers), with a head of dishevelled and agonizingly appealing blond hair. Daisy and I ached, we longed, we lusted for Mr. Grant.

Once or twice he brought his little daughter to school with him, because of some crisis at home — illness, the death of an in-law, failure to obtain a sitter. Her name was Abigail, and she was three years old. She would sit up at a little table which he'd brought along with him, cutting out shapes (badly), drawing scribbly, undecipherable pictures, leafing through a pile of picture books, sometimes talking out loud, but quietly, to herself.

From time to time, Abigail would stop to listen, or just to look — watching her father as he wrote assignments on the blackboard or described to us the social customs of the early Romans. She also scrutinized the students — solemnly, her eyes level and interested, taking it all in. She had blonde hair like her father's, curly like her mother's. Her large, blue eyes were framed by a fringe of dark lashes. She was very beautiful, and I admitted to myself that if Mr. Grant were to reject his wife and opt for me, I would be happy to accept Abigail as part of the bargain. In any case, it was clear that this would be necessary. Even while discussing the marriage rituals and dietary habits of the Romans, his eyes kept focussing on that little table, gazing at Abigail with a love that was public and poignant. I hoped he would look at my own children (*our* own children) in the same way.

One day, very late on a December afternoon, Daisy and I meandered home after basketball practice. We talked, laughed, complained about our parents, chewed gum loudly and with our mouths open, pulling long strings of it out at arm's length, and then tossing back our heads to reel it back in.

"Dis*gus*ting!" I said, through three separate wads of gum.

"But delightful," said Daisy, as the last grey strool of gum was sucked back in.

It was delicious to be out in the early evening now that the days had become so short. The heavy darkness of the blackout pressed in on us, but the rising full moon was beginning to pick up details in our surroundings. The edges of the Morrisons' silver birch were, indeed, silver. A ghostly blue light shone on the white wooden houses, the bare branches, people's faces.

A practice air-raid siren — which we'd learned to ignore — almost drowned out the scream of a fire-engine. But we heard it. A fire! Daisy and I were avid fire-watchers, and never missed a major fire unless extraordinary circumstances prevented us from attending — as when the Queen Hotel burned down during the week I had chicken-pox. But we could certainly enjoy this one. It was nearby. We could tell. The sirens had whined to a stop, and we could see a pink glow reflected on the Jacobsons' roof. A familiar eagerness squeezed my chest.

We didn't have to speak. In unison, we raced in the direction of the sounds of shouts, unreeling hoses, the clatter of ladders. And came to a stop, facing a four-story, box-like apartment building on a South End street. The firemen were already affixing hoses to the hydrant, racing in and out of the front door, shouting instructions and information to one another. The deepening red reflection on the Jacobsons' house was coming from the apartment building's third floor. Flames were visible behind three of the windows and belched out of a fourth, which was open. Bedraggled tenants were stumbling out of the side and front entrances, men staggering under the weight of valuables (I could see a painting of the Peggy's Cove lighthouse, a briefcase, a flat box for storing silverware, a stack of photo albums, a ragged-looking teddy bear), women carrying babies, children crying. On the fourth floor, windows were being shoved open, and smoke was starting to curl slowly through the openings and underneath the roof.

I grabbed Daisy's wrist. "Daisy!" I yelled above the din. "Mr. Grant lives in there!"

Daisy's fist flew to her mouth, and she shouted into my ear. "Yes! And on the fourth floor!" She'd gone there once to deliver an essay. We both stood unmoving, scarcely breathing, scanning the exits for the three familiar faces, watching the windows through the gathering smoke. Ladders were already being moved into place, to rescue a family that had appeared at a corner window. One by one they came down, agonizingly slowly.

Suddenly I clutched Daisy's arm again. "Look!" I whispered, and pointed to the middle window. There they were: Mr. Grant, his face frantic; his wife, her eyes wild; their screaming daughter. The ladders were in use elsewhere. There was nothing there for them. Between coughing fits, they called for help, and struggled to keep Abigail from racing back into the room. Then we could see the three of them leaning out beyond the windowsill, obviously trying to find some air they could hope to breathe, Mr. Grant holding Abigail as far out of the smoke as possible.

All of a sudden, one of the ladders slammed against the wall beside their window, jarring one of his arms loose from Abigail. For a long moment, he struggled to hold her with his free arm, unable to reach her with his other. Then, as if in slow motion (or so it seemed to me later), she slipped out of his grasp and started her awful journey to the pavement, far below. When she landed, she was as close to me as if she had been on the other side of my own living room. I heard the appalling sound as she struck the sidewalk. I watched it. I saw all of it, all the horror of what there was to see. When I tore my eyes away long enough to look at the window again,

Mr. Grant was gone. Where? He would never be able to get through that inferno of the third floor to reach ground level. But he did. He raced out the front door, fire licking at his trousers, his sleeves. Firemen had to stop him forcibly, in order to turn the hose on him to put out the flames.

Then he walked over to what was left of his daughter, slowly now, like a sleepwalker. He knelt down, picked up her body, and held it in his arms. Then he raised his head up to the sky, and made sounds that I had never before heard coming from a human being — long wails of anguish, like a large animal in mortal pain. I stared up at the window again. Mrs. Grant was being carried down the ladder by a fireman, draped like a sack of flour over his shoulder, her eyes closed.

By the time I looked again at Mr. Grant, someone had placed Abigail's body on a stretcher and covered it with a sheet. Mr. Grant was kneeling on the pavement, curled over with his head against his knees, pulling at his hair. The animal sounds continued, but lower, slower. Off to the side, I could see an ambulance attendant approaching him. Or a doctor, maybe.

By now, the entire building was ablaze. "C'mon," I croaked to Daisy. "I'm leaving."

On the way home, Daisy was full of talk. Agonized talk, shocked talk, but nonetheless talk. I thought I might kill her if she said one more word.

"Shut up, Daisy!" I shouted. "*Just shut up!*" Then I broke away and ran back to the school, stumbling over curbs on the street, and over bits and pieces of play equipment in the school yard. Finally, I found the little kids' jungle gym, and sat down underneath it, curled up in the fetal position, holding my chest with both my arms. I rocked back and forth, moaning rather than crying, my mind a confusion of images and fear.

I kept muttering over and over again, "Please, God. Please, God. Please, God." Please *what?* I had no idea.

After a time, with a kind of consuming fatigue that was new to me, I rose from my cramped position and stood up. The moon was well above the horizon now, and it was no longer difficult to see. Slowly I walked home, staring at the sidewalk, trying not to think, talking to myself. What I said was: "Empty. Empty. Empty."

When I opened up the front door of my house, there was visible relief on everyone's face, even on Jeremy's. Where had I been? Why hadn't I called? Didn't I realize how worried they'd be?

I realized no such thing. I cared nothing for their worry. I didn't answer them. I walked straight upstairs and lay face downward on my bed. I could hear my father outside my door, saying to my mother. "She saw it all. Daisy said so. No one should see anything like that at the age of fourteen. I think we should leave her alone for a while."

* * *

Mercifully, the next day was Saturday. It was therefore not yet necessary to face school and all the eager questions people would ask — with shock, with sorrow, with relish. Jeremy shut himself up in the den with his Meccano set. Obviously, he'd been warned to keep out of my way.

I looked with uncustomary fondness at my father, who was sitting in his favourite armchair, reading the *Halifax Chronicle.*

"I'm sorry, Dad," I said. It was the first time I had spoken since returning home the previous night.

He looked up, puzzled. "Sorry about what?"

"I'm not sure," I said. "About your war and all. Yes. About your war."

His brows were squeezed together, but he smiled at me.

My mother approached me with cornflakes, which I pushed aside. Not angrily. It was just that I knew I couldn't eat them.

"I know it was very bad," she said.

"Yes," I said. "It was bad."

Then I spoke again. "Mrs. Grant. Is she alive?"

"Yes," she said. "But in shock."

"Yes," I whispered. "In shock."

"Lisa," my mother said. "From our attic window, I can see a convoy going out. I know how you love to see them. Do you want to go up on Citadel Hill and watch?" I sensed that she could hardly bear to see me like this.

"No," I said. "Sorry, Mum, but I don't think I want the war today." Or maybe any other day, I thought. As I sat there in front of my uneaten cornflakes, I let the war go. I released it with reluctance, but I let it pass out of me and into some other space where it belonged. I was picking balls of fluff off my sweater.

"Sweetheart," my mother urged, voice low, eyes kind. "Would you like to talk about it?"

"Maybe sometime," I said. "Thanks, Mum, but right now I guess I'm not quite ready."

Then I went upstairs and lay on the bed for a long time, staring at the ceiling, thinking. After a while, I got up, crossed over to my desk, sat down, and started to do my history homework.

Over the Moon

Susan Adach

It happened on a night so long ago and far away, the memory should be no more than a smudge. It isn't. The events of that night are a series of vignettes constantly playing before my mind's eye. Taunting me.

Of course, this limp will never allow me to forget.

* * *

It was a heady day, the morning I arrived at the farm of the king. I had been chosen from cows across the land. A great honour had been bestowed upon me.

However, I should have been forewarned of danger by the absence of other cows in the barn. For a moment, I noticed no chewing of cud, no tang of cow scent, nor saw a single cow in any stall. By all accounts, I was alone.

But the sight of the place soon prevented any logical thinking.

It was a palace of a barn! Beds of heather as soft as angel hair. Walls of pearlescent marble. Troughs filled to overflowing with every delicacy — hot grain mush, nuts and apples, and carrots as thick and long as a bull's horn. Handsome servants stood at the ready, waiting to tend to every need. A true Eden if ever there was.

The king was there to greet me. He strode forward surrounded by a company of attendants.

"Welcome, my dearest cow!" he boomed, slapping my hind quarters. "Delighted to see you! I trust you will be comfortable here. Soon I will fill this barn with a bounty of bovine beauties from every corner of the globe. My herd will be the envy of all other kings." He stretched out his arms and waved them with a flourish. "To that end, I have built this barn, a structure worthy of cows of such exceptional breeding." His entourage nodded and smiled their agreement.

The king turned to the servant standing nearest who held a large cat and was stroking the long black fur. The cat looked perfectly content.

"Put down that mangy stray at once!" ordered the king, "Then take Diddle to his stall."

(Diddle: I was soon to learn from the plaque above my stall that this was to be my name.)

The servant immediately tossed the cat aside like a bucket of dirty wash-water and did as the king bade him. He secured me in my stall, covered me in a warm blanket, then returned to his post.

Satisfied, the king left in a flurry of robed escorts.

And so I remained, the sole occupant of these grand surroundings. Well, there was one other resident: the cat, a feline of no particular note. Unless you are taken by fur that gleams as black as the dead of night and eyes that penetrate to the very soul. I was not. Cat kept his distance. At least, he did until the third day after my arrival.

On this particular day, Cat sidled up to me accompanied by his insipid cohort, Little Dog, who lived in the palace with the king.

"Hey Diddle," Cat said. "Diddle." He nudged me with his claw. "It would appear you have settled in quite well."

Cat then leapt to the rail above my head. He stretched back on his haunches, rolled over to languish on his back. I plunged my muzzle deep into the trough.

"I would, however, feel remiss, Diddle, if I did not pass on this warning to you."

He gave a cursory glance about the barn, then lowered his voice to a conspiratorial whisper. "The night will come, Diddle, when you will hear the music of a fiddle and the clatter of a dish and spoon and — believe me, it pains me to tell you this — you will wish you never set hoof in this place."

Little Dog snickered.

Cat raised a paw for silence.

I lifted my head from the trough and rolled an eye on Cat. "Whatever do you mean?"

Cat's tail twitched. He licked his lips relishing the moment.

"I mean quite simply, dearest Diddle, that the king loves his beef." Cat eyed my flanks, "This barn is a sham! So heed my words! One night, as he listens to his favourite violin concerto, *Opus Boeuf 1,* his palate will cry out for the taste of ribs served hot and bloody. Down to the barn he will trot, dish and spoon at the ready, and you, my handsome heifer, will be ribs du jour!"

Cat uttered a sympathetic cluck of his tongue and shook his head. Without another word, he jumped from the rail to join Little Dog. The pair scampered from the barn, leaving me to tremble in my quivering skin.

The king would eat me! Troughs filled to the brim! Of course, to fatten me for the slaughter!

For two terror-filled nights I listened for the violin, the clang of the dish. Nothing was heard. I did my best to stay awake. But on that third and fateful eve, my lids did hover then close. Sleep was upon me in an instant.

It was a painful slumber, pierced by razorous nightmares. Kings playing violins . . . kings with violins for crowns . . . surrounded by dishes and spoons robed in dripping ribs . . .

I awakened at the sound of a violin. It cannot be!

The notes came at a feverish pitch. No, it's true!

I kicked at the door of the barn. Servants scrambled to block my way. I flung them aside. Bursting through the door, I heard the clatter of dish and spoon jangling in the distance. I galloped for open field, the rattle of tin on china plate and the screech of the violin hard upon me.

I leapt with fright into the star-filled sky, easing past the moon as I flew. I snatched a glance backward at the farmyard.

Little Dog rolled in the dust howling with delight.

He tugged on a rope strung across the farmyard. Affixed to the rope, a dish and spoon ran away over the yard, chattering madly.

And out of the shadows stepped the Cat — violin in hand, playing merrily.

Above the din, he shouted, "Adieu, my half-witted heifer! Fool! Had I known it would be so easy, I would not have waited three days to execute my plan. Remember this, you bovine buffoon, the barn is mine! It only and ever will be . . . Cat's!"

* * *

I landed in a field miles away. Hence the limp. I hobbled to a farm some distance down the road, a decrepit and drafty old place. The company was welcoming, the food plain but plentiful. And so I stayed.

A spring and summer had passed when I heard rumours over the fence that the infamy of that humiliating night had been immortalized:

> *Hey Diddle, Diddle*
> *The cat and the fiddle*
> *The cow jumped over the moon*
> *The little dog laughed to see such sport*
> *And the dish ran away with the spoon.*

Or so they say.

I do not believe it will last however.

Dead Jim

V.S. Menezes

I have kissed a dead guy, and Brad thinks this is fabulous, which is Brad and me in a nutshell.

I didn't even know Jim was dead until the next day at school when he didn't show up. At first this didn't mean too much. Jim sat in front of me in homeroom, and he was hardly ever there in the mornings anyway.

He wasn't a punctual guy. He was more a messed-up kind of guy, all thin and pasty from too much night groovy activity and too little food. This is what made him very attractive to both me and Brad. We love that pale, gaunt, barely-clinging-to-life look.

That's our style. A mix of glam, punk, goth. As long as it's black and strange. But our main fashion influence is film. The Charlotte Rampling in *The Night Porter* look. *The Edward Scissorhands* look — cuts included. The *Elvira, Mistress of the Dark* look, which is my favourite because of the bouffant hair and stilettoes.

Brad and I vie for the same guys. Brad is big into unrequited love, always on the brink of killing himself over some guy or other. The latest was Tony in The Bay's men's wear. Brad barricaded himself in the bathroom there one Saturday, threatening to kill himself if Tony didn't go out with him. Needless to say this only embarrassed Tony and got Brad thrown out by mall security.

Before Dead Jim, I had Brad drooling over Teddy, this hemophiliac boy I was seeing whose skin barely contained his blood. He was almost transparent, beautiful, and delicate. But his family was white trash — a biker guy and his babe, and this real bruiser of a brother.

Teddy had some kind of death wish — like he couldn't live with the closeness of death so he tempted it, going to beer parties with his killer brother or racing into the winter night without a coat, blind to the ice that could knock him down and slice him open.

I finally stopped seeing him because I couldn't live on that edge. Brad was disappointed. So I said *you* go out with him, which he tried, but the brother put an end to that.

So anyway, it's almost nine and Jim isn't here in homeroom, and I'm not thinking anything of it until Mrs. Glen says, "There will be an announcement in a few minutes and I want you all to know first. Jim Thomas died last night. He drowned."

Instantly I knew he'd drowned in the Jacuzzi in his parents' solarium. That's where we'd been. No, no, no. Not having some wild sex orgy. We'd just been sitting by the edge of the water, watching the outdoor lights reflect on the surface.

Brad and I have a spare right after homeroom and Brad is waiting by my locker, shaking with the news. Knowing Brad, he's trembling with excitement.

I'm not sure I'm so thrilled at this point. What if there's an investigation and I'm questioned. "You were the last person to see the deceased. Was he alive when you left him? What time was that? . . . " Next I'll be up for murder one.

We walk across the street to Sweet Nick's Café. Nick makes the other kids buy take-out and squat on the curb to eat. But Nick is European and he thinks Brad and I are artistes, so he lets us sit inside. He even refills our coffees for free.

"We intellectuals, we gotta stick together," he says. "Know what I mean?"

Brad and I always nod sagely when he says this, and let him blab on about politics for a few minutes. He offers us one of his cigarettes, then goes back to his post by the cash and listens to his opera.

Once we're safely huddled in the back corner under a cloud of smoke, Brad says,"I'm bursting. What was it like?"

"What was what like?"

"Kissing a man one minute and seeing him dead the next."

"He was alive when I left him. I swear. It's weird to think he's dead now. I didn't even know him that well."

Who did? Mostly he was just the guy everybody stepped over on the way to the student parking lot. He was always slumped in that doorway doped up and smoking, listening to his Walkman.

What did I even *see* in Jim. Maybe he reminded me of Teddy, only Jim didn't run headlong toward self-destruction — it was more like a side effect of achieving total oblivion.

"I just feel kind of bad that no one really cares, except that it's juicy to talk about. Not a whole lot of students just up and die. I bet no one even goes to the funeral."

"We can go," Brad says, perking up at this. He'd drifted during the sentimental stuff. "I'll bet they have an open coffin because he died in his youth. Tragically. At the peak of his beauty."

"Open coffins are so sick. I guess I could go, seeing I was the last one to see him, but what would we say to his parents if they're there."

"Well, maybe they won't be. But if they are, just mumble 'my condolences' and look sad."

"No rushing to the coffin to take a look," I warn Brad.

"So I guess that means we'll go."

"Yeah, we'll go."

* * *

I hate funerals. Like, who doesn't — except Brad. They remind me of when I was in eighth grade and my Great Aunt Elma died. This was my dad's aunt of the mauve hair and whimsies, which are these fancy hair nets she always wore.

Sometimes she'd sit in the living room and talk to me about the Bible. I always pretended to be interested. That would make her smile, and then I'd get to see the shiny plastic gums of her false teeth.

The day after Christmas, Mom, Dad, Elma, and me were driving home from my Aunt Millie and Uncle George's house. Everyone was laughing a lot because they'd all been drinking — even Elma. Then my Dad did one of those silent farts, and it smelled so bad, and we all thought this was the funniest thing because we had to roll down our windows, and it's like one in the morning and twenty below zero.

We get home and Elma drifts up the stairs to bed saying, "No one wake me up. I want to sleep in."

Then about eleven the next morning I'm sitting at my dressing table drawing on my eyebrows and my mother walks in. She's all white and she says, "Elma is dead."

Mom was in shock so I had to make all the calls and look after her until Dad got home.

Then it's all kind of a blur except seeing the coffin come down the stairs and that night I went to the show with my girlfriend Beth and two guys we knew. We sat through the feature twice. When we came out it was midnight and my dad was waiting on the deserted street, leaning against his car, the snow swirling around his legs. He was really mad.

He said to Beth and me, "Get in the car." And to the guys he said, "You boys get out of here."

I tried to say something and he said, "Shut up."

I guess there was a funeral and stuff, but I can't really remember. It's like I blocked everything else out from that moment. But I saw Elma's dead body lying in bed that day. She just looked asleep, so maybe when I see Jim he'll be sleeping too.

* * *

I feel kind of guilty about Great Aunt Elma's death. Like I should have been at home comforting everyone instead of going out with my friends, and I feel kind of guilty about Jim's death, too. Like if I'd hung around longer he wouldn't be dead.

But it wasn't like he begged me to or anything. He'd gotten a bottle of wine out of his parents' stash. He chugalugged right out of the bottle, then handed it to me. We were sitting on the floor, our backs against the glass of the solarium, our feet stretched out in front of us. Jim had his arm around me.

I'd had wine before and I'd necked before, too, which I figured we were leading up to, but I hadn't done both at the same time. I felt guilty like we might get caught, but Jim didn't seem to care. He said his parents never came home before nine, and if they did, they wouldn't say anything. I got the feeling they'd pretty well given up on him.

We kissed a few times, but then Jim seemed more interested in the wine than me, so I left. And now he's dead. I bet he got drunk and fell in the Jacuzzi. With all that metal he wore he'd have sunk to the bottom like an anchor.

So Brad and I go to the funeral parlour. Brad is in a black great coat even though it's summer. I'm in widow's weeds — a black crepe dress, a black pill box hat with a veil and a fox slung around my neck — you know, the kind with the teeth that clip to the tail. I'm wearing my hair in a chignon. My stockings are black cotton and my shoes are a pair of black orthopedics with stacked heels.

The funeral parlour is tucked between a strip mall and a car dealership in a newer subdivision that ate up the woodlands north of our burb. It's so weird to me that the developer took out every tree then had to plant these little sticks where there once was a whole forest.

Why am I thinking ecology when I should be thinking sad thoughts about Jim?

We go inside and it's all real posh and hushed. A very serious guy in a black suit ushers us past the Shady Grove Parlour and I almost think I see Elma sitting in the chair holding her Bible. But it's some other old lady looking all red-nosed and sad for the dead person in there with her.

We're directed to the Cedars Room. It's long and narrow with the coffin right up front. The parents — that's who I figure they are — are standing beside it. They're looking at us like this is a cocktail party and we're the guests.

Brad is walking real slow and sorrowful, but I can feel the tension in his body because I'm holding his arm — mostly to stop him from bolting up to the coffin and standing nose to nose with Jim.

The parents greet us.

"My condolences," I say.

Brad says the same thing, *very* dramatically, then gives his full attention to the deceased.

I'm shocked that Jim looks pretty much the same in death as he did in life. Pale skin and a black shirt. I figure he also has on black pants but I can't see. And he looks way better with his hair combed.

"You were friends of Jim?" his father asks.

"Yes." I smile. "I sat behind him in homeroom."

"How sweet of you to come," his mother says.

I smile again. She doesn't know I was there the night Jim died. And I'm not about to tell her. Except for Brad, no one knows I've dated Jim a few times and kissed him hours before he died.

It seems kind of sad to me that someone could live and die and no one would know anything about his life. I feel like I should say something, like how I was kind of Jim's girlfriend and how Brad and I always thought he was real cute. But then again, maybe some things are better left unsaid.

Peripheral Dreams

Alison Lohans

S tephanie blinked.

The stupor of sleep hung about her. A flute was playing a Handel sonata, probably the one in A minor. Grass teased her neck, trespassing the bounds of her tank top, tickling her armpits. Even the air was drowsy, ripe with summer. A tiny something was creeping across her right wrist.

She bolted upright, heart lunging.

She was alone. Just the poplar tree, and the grassy field.

Of course.

Afternoon sunlight and flickering poplar shade danced across her face and body. It must've been the sun that woke her.

She'd thought it would be easier, away from home. Even so, for the past several nights, thoughts of Trent had kept her shivering in her sleeping bag long after the other girls had finally drifted off.

She rubbed the nape of her neck, noting the soft fuzz and bristles, where only recently hair had streamed to the middle of her back. It still felt strange.

Shouts came from the recreation area, accompanied by the occasional high *thwokk* which suggested some of the kids were playing volleyball. Among the trees somewhere, the flute kept singing. It sounded like Angela.

Stephanie brushed dry grass from her shorts, from her legs. A flurry of pops chased the stiffness from her spine.

The Haydn concerto was surging in her mind; her fingertips twitched eagerly.

She'd practise for a while, and afterwards she'd sign up for the dinosaur tour.

* * *

In the small practise room, she drew her bow across the worn cake of rosin; she tuned, listening to the minute pitch discrepancies in the harmonics, adjusting the fine-tuners.

Alone. Her body was caught in an involuntary shudder.

She didn't know the kids here well. And they didn't know the Stephanie Vaughn of the trailing hair, whose secret ambition was to be the next Shauna Rolston. Nor did they know the frightened girl whose knotted insides kept her from chasing that dream.

Her insides, and Trent. Together, they'd built a thick glass wall that let her hear the music, but never let her *be* it.

Only a week remained before it was time to go back to Winnipeg. Soon after that, Trent would return from tree planting.

She attacked the G string on her cello, playing not the Haydn, but an angry improvised passage aimed far away.

The Yamaha upright piano in the tiny room sat forlorn, ignored. She almost felt sorry for it as the wild, undisciplined tune took her in unexpected directions.

The knock on the door came when she was playing a frenzied repeating pattern in fourth position on the A string.

Stephanie swore and got up. Her arm curled around her cello; she propped the endpin in a tiny gap between two floorboards so the instrument wouldn't go skating away from her. Rage was still spitting strong; it found a handy focus in the boy standing there in a grey T-shirt with Bach's face on the front, and scruffy cut-off jeans.

"*Sorry*," he said, before she'd said a word. "I was just wondering who wrote that piece."

"Nobody."

Probably half the kids here thought she was a conceited bitch. But so what. That was one advantage of going to camp out of province. Go for the superb musical instruction, don't play any stupid social games, and come home glad. Glad, for the music. For the unvarnished opportunity to be real for a change. Glad, especially, for the chance to be away.

He gave her a look, Owen Schwartz of the dark hair that tumbled in curls almost to his sholders, of the narrow face with green-grey eyes that gave the impression of seeing much more than actually seemed to be there. Owen Schwartz, who'd stunned the pants off the jury with his audition piece, an arrangement of a Frescobaldi toccata. Owen was principal cello.

"Nobody, eh?" he said.

Hugging her cello, she looked away. Her feet were bare; the left one was dirty so she tucked it behind her right, but that sent her off balance. "I was just fooling around. I was mad."

Owen apparently took this as an invitation; he came the rest of the way in, and plopped down on the piano bench. "I noticed," he said. "Think you could do it again, that same way? It was cool, the way you led into that second part."

The angry music still thundered in her head, but she knew it was hopeless. The connection was gone, that kinetic link between what she heard, and the answering response in her bow arm, and the fingers of her left hand. "I don't think I could do it again," she mumbled, sliding her fingertips over her cello. A tiny patch of dirt was crusted onto the glossy, varnished wood; she scratched at it with her fingernail.

"Mind if I try?"

Startled, she looked at him. It had been a long time since anyone had asked to play her instrument. In a way, it was an invasion. Almost like . . .

"That's cool," he said when she didn't respond. "I wouldn't let most people near my cello, either." And he stood up, his hand slapping a careless rhythm against the top of the piano.

"Wait." Her stomach somersaulted. "Here." And she thrust the cello toward him. If anything, it would be refreshing to see him fail. He *would* fail; she knew it; she could hardly remember what she'd played herself. Their hands brushed in the exchange, a quick touching at the cello's neck. His hand was dry, and warm. With her bare foot, she sent her beige carpet strip across the floor to him, so he could anchor the endpin.

"Thanks." He set one of the piano bench legs on the carpet, then lengthened the endpin on her cello; he twisted the screw on her bow until he was satisfied with the tension in the horsehair. He re-tuned.

His hair, longer than hers, jiggled slightly with every movement. She watched his intent face, which seemed to have secrets of its own. It was too intimate, the way his bare, hairy knees grasped her cello, the way the scroll brushed against his left ear. She wished she could take it back.

Sometimes Trent mocked her, claiming she looked like she was making out with her cello. Suddenly she understood, without wanting to.

She kicked her cleaning cloth against the closed door; it made a faint, whispered protest on wood.

Owen settled in, getting a feel for her instrument with the prelude of Bach's first cello suite, the one in G major. Her cello sounded different when he played it. Warmer. Brighter.

Stephanie slumped in the straight-backed chair. She watched his strong fingers dart across the fingerboard, watched his bowing wrist flex and relax with a breathtaking fluid motion.

If she still had her long hair, she'd twist the ends, keep herself occupied. Her head felt naked. Maybe it hadn't been such a great idea to get it cut, not so short, not right before camp. Except . . .

Owen stopped before sick jealousy set in. "How'd you start, anyway?"

Stephanie shrugged. The Bach had completely erased her own angry melody. Bach had a way of doing that, cleansing ugly feelings. "I forget," she said. "It's gone."

She watched as the boy leaned over her cello, almost as if he expected it to remember, and tell him. She watched as her bow glanced and glided across the strings, voicing melodic snatches that she recognized only for their not-quite-rightness.

Finally he shook his head. "I lost it, too." Their hands brushed again as he gave her cello back. "I'm sorry I interrupted you." His green-grey eyes said he meant it.

"It's okay. I was just fooling around." She looked away, repositioned the carpet strip.

"Stephanie?"

"What?" He had the door open now.

"I'm really sorry. I would've been pissed."

"It's okay; it wasn't important. I was just upset, that's all." Biting the inside of her lip, she waited for him to go.

But he didn't. "Have you been on the dinosaur tour, yet?"

The T-rex dig was bringing in tourists from all over. For it to be so close to camp was sheer coincidence, but a lot of kids were going during free time. It was a once-in-a-lifetime opportunity. She shook her head, and again missed her hair.

"Want to go? I'll pay — as if that could even begin to make up for your music . . . "

Her back straightened, the slightest bit. "Sure."

"I'll sign us up for tomorrow. If there's still room." His mouth curved into a half-smile; he gave a half-salute and was gone.

Trent would be furious. She loved it.

Instead of playing the Haydn, Stephanie clasped her arms about her cello, rested her head on its curved wooden shoulder. Pain gripped her by the throat.

She wept.

* * *

She avoided Owen later in the afternoon by ducking among the trees to write a letter to her friend Sarah while other kids went swimming or canoeing, or had jazz band practice. It was easy to avoid him at supper because her cabin sat in the southwest corner of the mess hall, and the guys sat mostly to the north. At evening choir practice it wasn't hard to avoid him because she was in the second row, and the basses were in back. During social time afterward, she stood alone on the pier, watching silver bleed across the lake, until a couple joined her, and started making out.

* * *

He caught up with her just after flag-raising the next morning.

Her eyes were scratchy, and she had a headache. Once she'd finally slept, after the panty raid that got as far as Willow cabin but not her own, Cottonwood, she'd dreamt of fighting off Trent. Of gripping him by the throat, sinking her thumbnails into muscle and sinew, ripping, while his eyes bulged in surprise.

Lying awake in her sleeping bag, heart pounding in her ears while leaves rustled outside and mosquitoes whined but never approached her repellent-drenched skin, she'd been horrified. And at the same time, fiercely glad, in a scary, crazy way. She felt like kicking the sagging lump in the bunk overhead that was Angela, to wake her up. It didn't matter that she hardly knew Angela; any sane human company would be welcome.

Later, when a severe thunderstorm rolled in and did wake everybody up, she'd been relieved. The blasts of light and noise, the whipping wind, and the heavy downpour all had a superb way of changing the subject.

Now red-and-white cloth snapped cheerfully overhead; the air smelled of moist earth. Kids were milling around before breakfast. Kendra, her counsellor and also a music major at the University of Regina, was talking with one of the other counsellors whose cabin had been raided, and the grim-faced director was hauling all the guys from Elm into the camp office, even shrimpy Jonathan who blushed and backed up if anyone female so much as looked at him.

Stephanie thought of her underwear, still tucked safely in her suitcase under the bunk. Waves of goosebumps scurried down her arms. Emily, who sat in front of her in orchestra, hadn't been so fortunate; her bra and a pair of lacy blue panties had been among the sodden assortment reeled down from the flagpole.

"Stephanie."

And so she turned, because there wasn't anyone else much to talk to. Today he was wearing a T-shirt that said *Sports suck — support an artist (me, for instance).*

Owen's greeny eyes crinkled with laughter. "Did your cabin get raided?"

"No." Her voice was cold.

His narrow face went blank. "I was only asking."

"It isn't funny." She fought the quick, bristling hostility. After all, he was innocent. Besides, supposedly they were going on the dinosaur tour. Momentarily she wondered what had happened at the dig site during the night's storm.

"Sorry. I didn't know you were such a feminist." He kicked a fallen poplar branch; laces trailed from his Lynx runner across the grass.

Something heaved in her chest. Stephanie looked at the branch while unexpected tears swam in her eyes, and the bright prairie morning swam about her. A feminist she was not. If she'd been more of one, she never would've gone out with Trent. At least, not a second time.

"It's okay," she said. "It just, kinda, freaked me."

An understatement, as she remembered huddling in her sleeping bag with dread sucking away her breath while the other girls whispered and giggled at the windows, and Kendra had parked herself outside the door, as if she could be an effective barrier against a bunch of high school guys gone wild.

"I got the tickets," he said after an awkward pause. "We go right after lunch."

"Thanks," she said, and meant it. Except she hoped he wouldn't expect anything more in return. She wondered if he even wanted to take her.

As everyone headed for the mess hall — except the guys in Elm — she wished she could crawl back into her sleeping bag. And sleep this time. Without dreams.

* * *

The morning breeze died during orchestra rehearsal. In the clearing among the poplars, the music sheets stopped fluttering, no longer needing clothespins to keep them from flying off the stands. Stephanie could sense the heat mounting as she struggled with a tricky passage in Tchaikovsky's *Swan Lake*; she was so tired it felt as if her bow arm were merely sawing the strings. In front of her, Emily appeared engrossed in the music, despite her lack of a bra. Beside her, stodgy Darryl sounded anything but musical. But that's the way it was, sitting at the bottom of the section.

She wondered if Shauna Rolston had ever sat last. Shauna, with her beautiful flowing hair, her deep involvement with the music; Shauna, who could send a cloud of rosin flying through the air on a powerful note. Stephanie knew, from sitting in the front row.

No, Shauna probably had always been at the top. Owen, too.

She looked at Owen's back, at his hair, at the scroll of his cello sitting alert beside his head. Leaf shadows flickered across him. She wondered if he had a girlfriend. Probably. But the sound of his cello . . . Even sitting at the fourth desk, with the basses directly behind her, she could hear his distinctive tone.

She could play like that; she knew it. If only . . .

Mr. Berg's baton slashed, cutting them off. This time he had something to say to the second violins. And, it turned out, to the flutes, who kept playing flat. Poor Angela.

Stephanie rubbed her bleary eyes, rested her head on her cello. After this, they had section rehearsals. She was so tired she'd probably do something stupid, like drop her bow. Then they'd all stare, and whisper.

She yawned. And wondered why the hell she'd agreed to go on a long hike to look at a bunch of old bones.

* * *

After lunch, they walked into town along a gravel road. With the heat of midday, there was no trace of the night's downpour. Owen was carrying a light pack.

She didn't know what to do with guys any more. Not now. Her throat knotted.

Owen seemed nervous, too.

Dust boiled into their faces as a pickup roared by.

It was good to melt into the anonymity of strangers, tourists with hats and cameras and canteens. Sitting in the tour van, they didn't touch, though Owen's bare knee occasionally glanced against hers when they hit a bump. Each time, she shrank away. Their silence was a bizarre pool of quiet in the midst of the banter of people come from all around to see the T-rex, and hear the running commentary by the guide. Owen was still wearing his *Sports suck* shirt; she wondered what people must think. She wondered what was in his backpack.

The rattly old GMC took them further and further out of town on gravel roads, passing grain and livestock farms, and skirting a small river valley. Outside, the world looked heavy with the heat of late July. Hawks glided lazily on air currents. A dead porcupine lay by the roadside and, later, a skunk fresh enough to leave a pungent odour, despite closed windows.

Stephanie's head ached. She felt a little carsick. The van kept turning onto narrower, dustier roads, until she was sure they must've somehow driven off the map. Or maybe across the border, into Montana. They clanked across a cattle guard, which rattled her teeth, and sent her swaying against Owen. "Sorry," she gasped.

He didn't answer.

They'd stopped. Fierce sunlight bounced off dry, grassy hills. Apart from human voices, the only sounds were the bawling of cattle, birds, and wind in the grass. The air smelled of sage, primitive, untainted. Stephanie wished she'd worn a hat.

As the sightseers filed into a ragged line for the hike to the dig, Owen pulled her aside. "What's the matter?" His face was tense; his eyes, more grey than green, opaque, seemed to understand nothing now.

She looked down at his hand, fingers clasping her forearm. Hesitantly, she pulled free while her heart thumped in panic. "It's nothing to do with you," she stammered. "I'm just kind of . . . stressed, that's all."

"I thought you wanted to see the dinosaur."

She could read the hurt anger from his voice without having to face those eyes. "I do." It came out wimpy, and false.

He swore. "What do you want to do, sit in the van? I didn't pay forty bucks just to . . . " He broke off.

Sweat trickled down the back of her neck. Forty dollars. He'd paid a lot of money, just for interrupting her in the practice room. Trent would've laughed, and called him a poor sucker.

She shook herself. "I want to see the dinosaur," she said. And she set off, walking quickly to catch up with the straggling end of the line.

* * *

Homemade signs marked the odd spot in the trail, cautioning them about hazards. *Beware of cacti and rattlesnakes,* said one. Beware of males, Stephanie thought. More dangerous than either of the above. She wondered if Owen, trailing behind her, would somehow find an opportunity to come in contact with her rear.

The trail grew steeper. It was very hot. She drooped, panting; she hadn't realized she was *this* stressed.

"Steph? You okay?" Owen wasn't even out of breath.

She took another step up the incline; her runner slipped, and for a dizzy moment she could see herself sliding downhill, rolling over one cactus after another. And maybe rattle-snakes.

But a hand caught hers and held the world steady, though dark spots swirled before her eyes, and her lungs gulped for air. "Are you okay?"

She nodded, and let him pull her the rest of the way up the trail.

It was a solemn, sad-looking heap that lay in a pit beneath their feet. The rust-coloured lumps protruding from earth and rock were not immediately recognizable as bones, and certainly not a dinosaur.

Stephanie sat on the dirt because she still felt shaky; after a moment, Owen sat beside her, and together they peered over the rim at the sight, at the helmeted paleontologists working away with picks and shovels. All around, people murmured and took pictures. Owen pulled a camera from his pack. With the movement, his shoulder brushed hers. She jumped.

One of the paleontologists began explaining, and slowly Stephanie began to see. With the rest of the tourists she craned her neck, looking up at the eroded hillside, at the layers of sediment, as their guide talked about iridium findings and coal seams. She followed the movement of the pick across the excavation, seeing now a femur, a rib, part of a jaw, another rib. Teeth.

It was all a jumble, body parts mixed together. The poor dinosaur had literally fallen apart.

The voice went on and people murmured, asking ques-tions; Stephanie propped her chin in her hands, almost seeing a living creature, a fierce, terrible lizard which, alive, would have sent all of them scampering for cover.

Now it was naked. Vulnerable. She wondered if its ghost lurked somewhere, minding the intrusion.

The sun shone hot on her naked neck, on her shoulders. She missed her hair.

Trent had been crazy about her hair.

Sad, vulnerable bones. Poked at, dug up. Examined by an alien species.

Hands. Grabby, hungry. Being touched, even if she didn't want it. Trent never listened. And the rest . . .

Something crumpled in her chest, in her throat. While the paleontologist kept talking, and tourists kept taking photos, something cracked in her gut. The dinosaur, the dirt, the sage smell in the air, they all blurred. She shrank away from a touch on her shoulder, tried to make herself small.

She ran. Blind.

Dirt, slipping beneath her feet. Falling, sliding; elbows slamming against rock, sharp spines clawing skin; falling; pain.

A stranger helped her up. He was in his fifties, probably. A man.

She yanked herself away, and slid further down the hill.

Sobbing uncontrollably now, she sensed people clustering about her. A spectacle, just like the dinosaur.

"Are you all right, dear?" A woman, this time.

"Stephanie . . . " Owen's voice. Poor guy; if he'd only known what he was getting himself in for . . .

She tried to stop crying but couldn't; the hurt inflicted by Trent was just too much. The emotional game-playing, like cat and mouse. The unwanted fondling, and worse. She sat up, scraped, bruised. Dirty. Her gut heaved. In fact . . . She lurched to her feet and darted through the small crowd. Safely into a little coulee, she dropped to her hands and knees and vomited, until she was sure that on the next retch, her stomach would come spewing out.

A woman came to sit with her as she quivered, handed her a dampened cloth to wipe her face, and helped her pull the prickles from her skin and clothing, all the while murmuring reassurances.

When the worst was over, Stephanie walked with the woman back to the parking area. Two of the tour vans had already left, and the remaining sightseers waited, some sitting with tinned soft drinks, some snapping photos of the low, treeless hills. Or of each other.

A solitary figure leaned against a fencepost overlooking dry range land. The back of his white T-shirt and cutoffs were caked with dust. On the other side of the barbed-wire fence, short-horned Herefords grazed.

Poor Owen.

He might never want to lay eyes on her again. But even so, she owed him an explanation. How much she'd tell him about Trent, she didn't know; she hadn't told anybody. Not yet.

She was still very shaky, inside and out.

But something felt different.

It took her a moment to figure it out.

The glass wall. It was gone.

The sage smell all around drew the world into a sharper focus. A slight breeze traced against her cheeks, whispered about her neck. She looked up into the summer sky where swallows swooped and dipped, their liquid voices fading, then swelling, as they circled.

Stephanie gathered it all to her with an indrawn breath, and then another.

Maybe now, she'd be able to play. *Really* play. Like Owen.

And maybe someday, like Shauna Rolston.

As she drew nearer, a sudden lightness danced in her chest, rising into the new, open cavity of her throat.

Owen Schwartz was whistling Bach to the cows.

The Pig's Elbow

Karleen Bradford

A s Emily pulled around the corner she could see Luna standing in front of the store, arms akimbo, staring at the front window.

She doesn't like it, Emily thought. Fine. Okay. Neither do I.

She'd been so excited when Luna had called her up two weeks ago. It was her first commercial art job. Now she couldn't summon up any enthusiasm for it. It wasn't just that she couldn't seem to come up with any original ideas and the work wasn't going well. It wasn't even that at all, if she was going to be honest about it. She closed the door in her mind that led to the real problem. She wasn't going to think about it.

Luna made a strange figure, standing there like that on the quiet, dusty, small-town street. She was a very large woman, made even larger by the voluminous, brightly-coloured caftan she wore. She was a spot of almost excruciating brightness in the hot summer glare. Her store wasn't exactly the kind of store you would expect to find on this kind of a street, either.

The Pig's Elbow.

"Where did you ever get that name?" Emily had asked.

Luna had shrugged and flipped her long, heavy braid back over her shoulder with a toss of her head, setting earrings dripping with silver and beads to jangling. "Crazy, isn't it? It just came to me. In a dream. And I want you to do something really wild for the sign. Something . . . creative, you know?"

There was a huge front window, filled with every kind of stuffed pig you could imagine. Mostly pink. Inside the store Luna sold other stuffed animals as well, but in the window it was all pigs. There was a broad band of bricks across the top that Emily had already painted periwinkle blue. She had spent all day yesterday lettering the store's name and surrounding it with dancing pink pigs. They looked ridiculous. Pathetic.

"Your mom let you have the car? Great!" Luna waved to acknowledge Emily as Emily pulled into the curb, but she was staring at the artwork. There was a slight frown on her face. Her mouth didn't look happy.

"I don't know," she said as Emily got out. "It looks . . . ordinary?"

"It looks awful. I know. Don't worry, Luna, I'll start over." With a sigh, Emily opened the trunk of the car and reached for the periwinkle blue paint. Good thing she had a lot of it. Looked like she was going to need it.

She'd been working for about an hour, standing on an old wooden chair that Luna had unearthed from somewhere, when she sensed he was beside her. She stopped painting and waited for him to speak. A strand of hair fell across her face, half-screening it. She didn't look at him.

"I didn't send the forms in yet," he said. "I really want you to talk to me about it, Emily."

She didn't answer. As long as she didn't say anything, he couldn't believe she was stopping him from going, could he? "This is such a great opportunity for me, Emily. I never thought I'd get the scholarship when I applied, you know that. You know I only applied for the stupid thing because Mr. Evans wouldn't get off my case about it . . . " His voice petered out.

He was waiting for her to answer. To give permission. To make it all right. To say that everything they'd been planning for the last three years didn't matter any more. She obliterated the last pig with periwinkle blue.

"Emily? . . . "

She got down off the chair and went over to the car. She put the blue paint back and reached for the pink. The paint at the far end would be dry enough to start outlining over it again. What could she draw on it this time? Singing pigs? Pigs jumping rope? Pigs waving their elbows in the air? Did pigs even have elbows? She moved the chair back to the other end and climbed up on it again.

"Emily?"

She slashed a line of pink onto the blue.

He left.

By the end of the afternoon, Emily had sketched in a number of pigs doing a variety of unlikely things. Luna had come out once to look, but had gone back in without saying anything. Her mouth still didn't look happy. At four o'clock, Emily gave up.

"I'm going, Luna," she called out. "See you tomorrow."

Home was down the road, just past the junction with the Toronto highway. Emily drove automatically, keeping her mind on pigs. Off everything else. She almost passed the boy without seeing him. Then his small, straight, solemn-faced figure registered. He was young, probably about nine or ten, but what made her take notice was the way he was dressed. In an old-fashioned tweed jacket, buttoned up to a high-necked shirt collar in spite of the heat. He had matching tweed pants, sort of full and gathered into a band below the knees. The word "knickerbockers" sprang into her mind, she couldn't imagine from where. A matching tweed cap with a peak over his eyes. High, laced-up black boots. He was holding out his

thumb in a classic, but oddly formal hitch-hiking pose. There
was a bicycle lying on the ground beside him.

Emily pulled over onto the shoulder and stopped before
she realized what she was doing. Never pick up hitch-hikers.
It was rule number one if she was going to borrow her mother's
car. But this was just a kid. And there was something about
him . . .

"Want a ride?" she heard herself asking.

He nodded, big-eyed, at her. "Just a ways," he said.

"Hop in, then. Where do you want out?" she asked as she
pulled back onto the road.

"I'll show you," he answered.

They reached the Toronto turnoff.

"There," the boy said, pointing. "By the bear."

Emily looked where he indicated, startled. Since when was
there a garage with a bear in a cage beside it on this road? Not
quite believing what was in front of her eyes, she parked the
car. The garage looked as if it was closed. There was a bulb-
headed gas tank in front of it. Emily stared at it. She had seen
an old tank like that somewhere before, but not one with gas
still in it. You could see through the glass top of this one and
it looked half full.

"I always come and feed him. Every day. But my bike
broke." The boy was walking towards the cage.

"Be careful . . . " Emily began. Surely this was against the
law. The cage had only a single set of bars; the bear could reach
out of it easily. "Watch out!"

But the boy approached it with the confidence of one who
had done this often. He held out what looked like a chunk of
brown bread. The bear stuck out his nose, snuffled at the
offering, then took it and swallowed it in one gulp. It snuffled
again at the boy's outstretched hand.

"He's hungry. They don't feed him too good," the boy said. "That's all I can give him, though. All I got." He sat down on a low stone wall, eyes fixed on the animal in the cage.

The bear dropped back onto his haunches. Emily could see now that his fur was matted. The concrete floor of the cage was filthy. There was a rank, strong, animal smell coming from it. The bear watched the boy hopefully for a moment, then heaved a huge sigh and dropped its head down between its paws.

"This is awful," Emily said. "They can't cage a bear up like that! There's hardly enough room in there for him to stand up!"

"I want to let him go. I even asked." The boy nodded toward the gas station. "But they told me to mind my own business. Said it brought a lot of customers in."

Emily sat down beside him. There was something really wrong about all this. She could vaguely remember her parents talking about a bear that had been caged around here once, but surely that had been a long time ago. When they were kids. She'd certainly never seen one before.

"You can go if you want," the boy said. "I can get home again from here."

"You sure?" Emily asked. She was oddly reluctant to leave him.

"Sure," he said. He had his eyes fixed on the bear, but the bear was staring at the line of trees just beyond him.

* * *

Work didn't go any better the next day. The pigs looked flat and boring. They didn't look like they were having any better a time than she was. After one quick glance at them and at Emily, Luna stayed inside.

He turned up soon after she started.

"The deadline's the day after tomorrow," he said. "I don't know what to do, Emily."

Maybe if she made them cross-eyed?

"Damn it, Emily, talk to me! Tell me what to do!"

It wasn't her decision. It was his. She wasn't going to say a word. It was up to him to decide whether he wanted to throw away everything they'd had together. Ever since they were fourteen. They'd always known they were meant for each other. Always known what they were going to do. He'd take over his dad's hardware store and she'd take art courses at the local college. They had it all planned out. Three kids, even. They'd always known. How could he even think of going away? That would be the end of it, she knew. He'd meet other people, do other things. That would be the end of it. But she wasn't going to stop him. If he wanted to go, he could go. She wouldn't say a word.

The boy was there again when she drove home. Somehow she had known he would be. She stopped and he hopped in without waiting for the invitation.

"I've got a doughnut for him today," he said. "He especially likes doughnuts."

He fed the bear, and they sat down together to watch him lick the chocolate icing off his snout. Even while eating, the bear didn't take his eyes off the woods on the other side of the road.

"I've got a plan," the boy said. "Tomorrow."

"What kind of a plan?" Emily asked.

"You'll see," he answered.

* * *

Emily persevered with the pigs, but the more she painted, the worse they looked.

"I didn't send the forms in."

Emily's hand took a wobble and one pig lost an eye. She dared a look at him, but wouldn't speak yet. Not yet.

"I don't think I will."

He wasn't looking at her. He was staring off into the distance, down the street. She turned his words over in her mind, weighing each one of them. He wasn't going to do it. He wasn't going to go. And he couldn't blame her. She hadn't said a thing to stop him.

He turned and left then, shoulders hunched.

She decided to take one of the stuffed pigs home with her that night. Maybe if she stared at it long enough, some kind of inspiration would come to her. When she saw the boy, she slowed and pulled over for him. He seemed excited.

"Look," he said as soon as they'd fed the bear. A bread and butter sandwich this time. He pulled out a small metal file from his pocket. "I'm going to file through the lock. I'm going to let him go."

Emily looked at the padlock on the cage door. It was old and rusty, but the hinge was thick. Much too thick for that tiny file. She didn't say anything, however, just watched as the boy set to work.

Half an hour later, the file broke. There was only a scratch to show on the padlock for all his effort. The boy dropped the broken pieces onto the ground. He sank down beside her.

"I'm not going to be able to do it, am I." he said. It wasn't a question. "I'm not going to be able to set him free."

That bear her parents had talked about. She remembered now: it had died, they had said. Sick and old and lonely.

"No," she said to the boy. "You can't set him free."

She got up, went to the car, and got the pig. It was a stupid thing. Useless. But she couldn't think of anything else to do. She held it out to him. He took it. As she drove away, she looked back. He was standing there, much as she had first seen him, straight-backed and solemn-faced in his tweedy, old-fashioned clothes, but with the violently pink pig under his arm. He waved. A small farewell motion. It would have been a silly picture if his face hadn't held the desolation of the world in it.

* * *

The next day she splashed periwinkle blue paint over the bricks and started again. She worked without stopping while the sun rose and while it began to set. At last, she was finished. She stepped off the chair and stood back to look. Luna came out of the store to stand beside her. She heard Luna draw in her breath.

"Yes," Luna said. "Oh, yes! I don't know what in the world you mean by it, but — oh my — *yes!*"

A small, straight-backed boy in old-fashioned tweed clothes, with an improbable pink pig under one arm, was waving to a bear. A glossy, fat, and beautiful bear. A bear that was running free and heading at a lope towards a thick woods. The boy was laughing; his face was full of joy.

Emily wiped her fingers off one by one. She stacked her paints carefully in the trunk of the car.

"Want a cup of tea to celebrate?" Luna asked.

"No," Emily answered.

It was time now.

Finally.

It was time to talk.

Deep Freeze

Diana C. Aspin

It was ten years ago when I saw them by accident, my dad and the woman. I was walking home from my friend Carolyn's fourteenth birthday party. I'd called Mom to remind her I'd be late.

"Don't worry, Alison, your dad will be late too," she'd said. "He's catching up on paperwork."

We were in the middle of a deep freeze. I stopped to look up into a crab-apple tree, its branches sleeved with ice and glistening like bones in the light cast by the street lamp. As I set off again I glanced over at the house.

On the porch a man was kissing a woman goodbye. He pulled her into him in a passionate way — like in the movies — and then he released her. The woman touched the man's cheek and when he turned to leave I realized, with a shock, that it was my dad. I ducked behind the tree, held my breath.

I watched my dad bounce off his heels as he walked down the street, his hands stuffed deep into his overcoat pockets. At the corner he turned and disappeared. As I stood there the screen door clicked open and a girl came out hauling a garbage bag. She headed for the curb. I supposed she was the woman's daughter. She was a few years older than me, slim with blunt-cut blonde hair which rose and fell into the nape of her neck as she walked. She had an air of confidence I would have killed for.

My heart pounded. I said, over and over to myself, there just *has* to be a mistake. I knew all about divorce and separation and affairs, but they were things that happened to other families. You have to understand that I didn't believe my father was like other fathers. He was a psychologist; he rambled on about communication and meaningful relationships, honesty, coming from a place of honour in all you do. My arms and legs felt numb, as if they didn't belong to me, and my stomach muscles kept tightening.

* * *

When I was growing up my dad's nickname for me was Ginger. Not just because of my hair, which was chili-pepper-red like his, but because of a ballroom dancer called Ginger Rogers. My dad fell in love with Fred Astaire and Ginger Rogers movies when he was a boy. In the movies Fred Astaire and Ginger gaze longingly into each other's eyes. Then they spin off, Ginger's dress, delicate and see-through as spider thread, opening and closing like a flower around her calves. Her throat is pale, her river of red hair cascades down her back. I guess when I was born and my dad peered into my hospital crib he couldn't believe his luck that I had red hair and he could call me Ginger.

My mom, who put up with all the romantic nonsense, was not a bit like Ginger Rogers. She was short and plump, like me, with a pretty face, and her black curls fit her head like a cap. She was — still is — an emergency room nurse and is extremely practical. It was convenient, her being a nurse. There was the time my dad caught flu. I remember him lying in bed and her leaning over him, stroking his forehead with a cool cloth. "My wounded soldier," she whispered. It was even handier when I fell off our swing set and my leg split open and globules of yellow fat oozed out. Other moms would have fallen into a dead faint. Not mine.

* * *

A few hideous days after seeing my dad with that woman, I raided his closet. In our house we respected each other's privacy, but I reckoned that when my dad decided to cheat on us he forfeited that right and the right to anything else besides. I wasn't sure what I was looking for, a clue maybe. I dug about in the pockets of his suits, but there was nothing there — no love letters or lipstick-smudged tissues. My fingers trembled and my heart banged like a drum. Then I pulled out the sleeve of the old blue shirt he wore when he was doing odd jobs about the house. I lifted it up and buried my face in it, took a deep breath. A mix of aftershave and deodorant, a pine scent that was exactly him. Some sadness, a feeling of something missing or irretrievably lost bubbled up, but I stuffed it back down.

I think that in some weird way I was looking for my dad in that closet, looking to find out who he was, where he'd gone. More than that, though, I see *now* that I was looking for me.

You see, the way I knew myself back then was through other people's reactions to me. Like, my dad was a mirror and what I saw in his reflection was a girl worth loving and living with and dancing with, a girl worth a nickname like Ginger, after a dancer he adored. After I saw him with that woman, spending time in that other girl's house instead of mine, I saw in the mirror a girl worth throwing away. I know that's not how *he* saw it but that's how it appeared to me.

I didn't find either of us that day. The sleeve, when I lifted it to my face again, was flat, shapeless, empty.

* * *

"Hi, Ginger," my dad said a week later, popping his head around the door of my room. Under my bare feet the floor vibrated with noise from my stereo. I'd developed a taste for sound that shook my walls and reverberated through my feet. Music which drove away all other sensation.

I pretended not to hear him. I just kept on rubbing the blood-red polish off my nails, driving the reddened remover into the clumps of chewed-up skin around my nail.

"I said: Hi, Ginger," my dad said.

I smashed the bottle down on my bedside table. Remover shot all over the wall. I rolled my eyes and rubbed furiously at my thumbnail.

"Look what you've done!" he exclaimed. "I don't know what's gotten into you lately." He left, came back with a wet cloth and began dabbing at the wall.

"Want to talk to your old dad about it?"

I stared at him blankly. He had a worried crease in the centre of his forehead, between his eyebrows, like a "V". In the old days — because now my life was suddenly divided into two distinct parts: then, when he loved us, and now, when he didn't — in the old days if I saw his worried "V", I'd tease him out of his mood. "How about it, Fred!" I'd shout, shaking my hair down my back. My hair was down to my bottom; it took a lifetime to grow it that long.

"Hey, what's up?"

I yanked my eyebrows up into a bored arch and one corner of my mouth down into a sneer. "Nothing. Is there anything *you* want to talk about?" I glared down at my nail.

"Me? Why?"

I looked up at him. His "V" had deepened; he really didn't get it. He really thought he could do this to us and get away with it. Liar. Cheat. I hated him. Let him suffer and die.

In the end he just barked, "Oh, I give up, Ginger!" and stormed out. It must have made him feel real bad to lose it like that. Being a psychologist and all.

"And don't call me Ginger any more," I screamed after him. "I *hate* that name! I *hate* it! I'm not a baby you know!"

"What was all that shouting at your dad about, Alison?" my mom asked the next day as she sat on the bed tugging on her white stockings. I was lying on her bed surrounded by my history books, ready to tackle my project after she left. She stood and slipped her feet into her white shoes. "Ugly uniform," she said, pulling down her slip, and examining herself sideways in the mirror. She ran her hand over her tummy, patted it as she would a friendly dog. "Not what it used to be," she said, kind of wistfully.

Ever since I was little it was my habit to lie on the bed and watch her get ready for work. I knew her routine off by heart: she showered and then appeared naked in a cloud of steam and the scent of Johnson's Baby Powder and dressed for work. She used to be thin as a blade of grass. You should see her in our old photos and Super 8 movies, her long, dark hair tied back with a ribbon, always smiling. Usually Dad was taking the picture and I was on her knee or hanging onto the hem of her dress. I guess we were her whole life, me and Dad. Oh, and her job in the emergency room and her garden full of wild flowers: sunflowers and columbine and blood-red poppies wide as dinner plates. In the summer her nails were always full of dirt from her scrambling about on her hands and knees weeding and feeding and planting.

I suppose you could say it had been too good to be true, our lives, too much like the Cleaver family. Something was bound to go wrong.

And it did.

"What was all that shouting about?" my mother repeated.

I shrugged. "Nothing."

Over the next week I lived in my room, reading and playing records, chasing away thoughts about the blonde girl I'd seen, the woman's daughter, hauling garbage to the sidewalk. The image of her was printed on the backs of my eyelids and

formed when I closed my eyes at night. I saw my dad leaving
us and leaning across her kitchen table, his shoulder brushing hers as he helped her with math. I saw her smile up at
him as he arrived — lips that parted to reveal those sicken-
ingly white, varnished teeth like you see on the cover of
Seventeen magazine. One night my imaginings got so bad that
I fished my old bear, Arnold, out of my closet. I tucked my
knees to my chest and pulled Arnold's head up under my
throat, pressed his fragile heart against mine. I cried and
cried until my head ached and I thought I'd never be able to
stop and Arnold's chewed-up ears were sopping wet.

A few days later things came to a head. My dad had promised
he'd be home early because there was an old Ginger Rogers
movie on at eight.

At seven-thirty he called. "Out of town? Oh, Greg, how
disappointing," my mom said. "We were looking forward to
watching *Carefree*, remember? Sure you can't postpone it?"
Then she nodded again and said, "Well . . . see you in the
morning. Bye."

Mom brought in buttered popcorn and we watched Fred
and Ginger do their stuff, Ginger's white gossamer scarves
fluttering from her wrists and shoulders, shivering carelessly
against her cheek. Mom wasn't in the greatest mood. She was
sewing a button onto Dad's shirt sleeve and she drove the
needle through the button and dragged it out the other side
over and over without looking at the television once.

I sat there ready to blow a gasket. She was always looking
after things — us, her garden, my gran, her patients. There
were dark circles under her eyes I hadn't noticed before.

Something inside me snapped.

I raced up the stairs two at a time. My heart thumped as I
snatched a carton of eggs from the fridge and some scissors
from the kitchen drawer.

"Where on earth are you going, Alison?" my mom shouted. I heard her coming up the stairs. "Alison, please come back."

"Won't be long, Mom!" I yelled. I knew that what I had to do would not take long.

* * *

I crouched down behind a snow-covered bush. I hurled an egg, sent it spinning toward the woman's screen door. It was a hit. Then I fired another one and another one, the hate now, after all those weeks, rising in my throat until I thought I would choke on it. Stupid! Liar! One egg after another. Cheat! Die! Until the door opened.

The woman my father had kissed so eagerly stepped out until she was standing directly under the porch light. She pulled her cardigan about her and stared at the smashed eggs plastered across the door. "What on earth . . . " she began. If I'd had an egg left I'd have thrown it at her.

"What is it?" It was my father's voice.

"Oh, look, Greg!" she exclaimed. Her voice rose an octave and broke on the word "look." I loved it, that breaking sound. I wanted all of her to break. Who did she think she was to take my father away from me! I wished her dead.

My father wore blue jeans and a white shirt. I remember thinking he must have sneaked them out of the house. "Who'd do a thing like that?" he said, staring at the carpet of egg shells and the gooped-up door.

I pushed myself up from my haunches.

"Me!"

I waited for him to lose it again, to rush down the porch steps and shake me, but he just stood there, frozen under the light. They both did.

The woman had straight brown hair, large eyes — but that could have been fear; I could taste and smell their fear and it made me feel strong. I stood my ground. I waited for him to make a move.

"Go in, Eva," he said to her eventually.

For a moment I thought the woman was going to speak to me, but she just put her hand across her mouth then went inside.

My dad sat down on the porch steps. He placed his head in his hands and left it there. My teeth began to chatter.

"It's nothing to do with you, Alison. You have to under-stand that."

"She's an ugly *cow*."

He looked up and I knew, even though there was a whole world of dark driveway and bush between us, that there was a deep "V" between his eyebrows.

"Alison . . . " he began. "Alison, I'm sorry . . . I don't know what to say."

"I do! She's a *fat cow*!"

I knew I'd cry if I mentioned the girl who was probably, at that very moment, somewhere inside listening to my childish outburst.

I squeezed my fists together and curled my toes up in my boots but the tears came anyway.

"I hate you! You're a . . . you're a . . . " I clenched my teeth, pulled my fists up level with my ears and shook them. "You're a baaaastard!" I screamed it so loud and long that a door sighed open on the porch of the next house then shut again.

"Oh god, Alison," my dad said.

I knelt and groped around under the bush for the egg box. I'd missed one cracked egg which was glued into the box. I threw it. It struck his shoulder and opened up, yolk and shell sliding down his arm. I took the kitchen scissors out of my pocket and brandished them in the air.

"Put those down!" he yelled, jumping up. "*Now!* I mean it, Alison."

I dragged a handful of hair from under the collar of my coat, tipped my head to one side and chopped it off at about shoulder length. The sound of the blunt scissors chewing through my thick hair made a sort of grinding noise and I half-expected it to hurt. It didn't. My whole life I'd been growing it, he knew that. He loved my hair. I grabbed another handful and did the same thing.

"I'm going home," I said, stuffing the scissors back into my pocket so hard the points pierced its lining. "And don't you *dare* follow me. I'm through with you. *Forever!*" I felt heat flood my cheeks and race across my scalp. Then, still choking and crying, I turned and ran, a slight breeze shifting the ice-slicked tree branches, rattling them like tin foil. I ran, crying, not looking behind to see where he was. I tripped headfirst on a mound of ice and grazed my palms as I slid along the ground.

In the den I stood shivering and sobbing.

"Alison!" my mom said. She scrambled up, her sewing basket spilling pins, buttons and thread. She flipped my hands and stared at my bloody palms. "What happened? Where have you been? And look at your hair!" She picked a clump off my shoulder and stared at it. The stink of the raw egg on my hands permeated the air.

"Are you all right?" Her voice shook and her eyes filled with tears. "I'm so sorry," she whispered. "I hadn't wanted you to find out."

* * *

Mom was tidying my hacked-up hair when he came in. I heard his heavy footsteps on the stairs. We both looked up as he came into my room.

"Alison tripped on the ice, Greg."

I don't know how she could stand to speak to him.

I narrowed my eyes and stared out at our maple. Its branches were sleeved with ice, just like the tree I stood under and watched my father and that woman the first time. It was hard to believe, right then, in the middle of the deep freeze we were in, that warmer weather would come, that those frozen branches would soften and bend with the weight of new leaves.

"I'll leave her to you," my mom said, brushing by him. "You make it right," she whispered harshly.

Music floated up from downstairs. Ginger, forever young, was spinning up a blur, her sequinned dress opening and closing, her river of red hair flowing.

"Alison . . . " my dad said in a pathetic attempt to make it right, "Alison, it's over."

I wanted to scream at him that it would never be over. He should know that, sitting like he did, day after day, watching crazy people weep and tear at their hair. He of all people should know that you can't just say, "It's over," and expect it to be over. If things could be over, bang, just because someone said so, or wanted it to be, he wouldn't have a job.

Eventually, because he refused to leave, I turned to face him. I could tell from the lines carved each side of his mouth, turning him suddenly old, that he knew there was no going back.

My dad reached out, placed his hand on the door frame, then pressed his forehead gently against it. He closed his eyes.

It was strange and awful what the sight of him, broken, did to my heart. My heart rose out of my chest and caught in my throat. For a split second, that's all, a split second, I wanted to hurl myself at him.

I knew just how it would be, my cheek turned softly against his shirt; I knew the scent of pine, knew exactly the amount of warmth I'd feel. I knew the exact spot to press my ear to listen to his thumping heart.

One day I'd lay my cheek against his chest again, listen to his heart, breathe in his scent, yes. But right then I was like that tree out there, sleeved with ice, frozen solid. I could not move.

"It's over. It's over," he said again.

* * *

And, as far as I know, it was over. Ten years later and I'm in my final year of post-grad studies — psychology. I'm at the kitchen window watching Mom attack her perennial border. Dad is mowing the lawn. His Walkman is on and he's lost to the world, cutting a circle around our old weeping willow. Any moment now Mom will peel off her flowered gardening gloves, slap them down on the grass beside her, place her hands in the small of her back and have a good stretch backwards before staggering to her feet. Dad will cut the mower and wipe his brow with the back of his hand. I'll walk out with the lemonade I just made balanced on our old wooden tray Gran bought for them before I was even born.

Yet I wonder as I step out with the lemonade, right this moment, smiling, at how little any of us know about those close to us. Was that woman the light of my father's life? Where is she now? Did he give her up for me? Was my mother's heart broken? How much does she hurt still? I'll never know. But this much I do know and it is more than enough. I know we are moving toward each other, drawn by habit and by history — and by the light and dark of that history — and above all, yes, above all by love. There is nothing to forgive.

Comes a Time

Robert Morphy

I t took some time to find it. Behind some weathered boards in a corner of the garage — a shovel. With the tool in hand Allan headed down the back yard to a place where there was a slight depression, well away from the trees that grew at the end of the property. He speared the shovel into the ground and knelt to put a tape into his portable cassette player: Neil Young's *Comes a Time*, his favourite.

The guitar and voice twisted toward him in the slight breeze as he stood and took up the shovel again. He glanced back at the house — his father in the kitchen window, a glass of rye and Coke in his hand. The shovel blade cut into the thick grass and he stood on it to drive it deeper. Then he made another cut, at right angles to the first. He planned to remove the sod in strips, so that it could be replaced, somewhere.

The work was heavy going. He felt somehow that the grass was tensing against him; that each severed yellow-white root was exacting a price. By the time he had removed several square metres, the sweat had begun to stand out on his forehead and he paused to take off his shirt. He knew that his father would be watching still and he could hear his voice: "Get some sun on that back! It'll get rid of those pimples."

His father had a thing about pimples. He'd had a lot of them himself when he was growing up — his face and neck were scarred — and he had a million theories about how to get rid of them. Allan had red patches on his back where liquid nitrogen had been applied "to kill bacteria". He would never take his shirt off at school.

He continued removing sod until he had exposed a three metre circle of earth. Half a worm writhed near one edge, and a squadron of ants fanned out to survey the damage. He stood for a moment and looked at his hands. There were red patches at the base of several fingers; a water blister marked the base of one. He thought about going into the house for a pair of gloves. Where had she left them, his mother?

No, he would do without gloves. He didnt want to talk to his father again, not now.

He returned to the centre of his patch and plunged the shovel in again. The earth was still dense with roots, but as he worked it began to come away more easily and soon he had a mound growing on the north side, away from the house.

The tape had run through twice. He liked the replay feature on his blaster, although it had driven his mother crazy. He had all of Neil Young's tapes and the Crosby, Stills, Nash, and Young tapes, and he played them in his room while he did homework or read. When he was absorbed in a book, he would set the machine on replay. He marked his progress by the number of pages read before a song came around again.

Today was Sunday. His mother had left on Friday. There had been letters for his father and for Allan on the kitchen table. Allan's had been opened before he got home. It sat on top of the envelope where it had been dropped, and Allan's father had stood at the window, a drink in his hand.

"She wants to live with that prick Macmillan," his father slurred. "Couldn't even talk to me about it — just ran off with that prick."

Allan had taken his letter out to the back yard. He read it by the light from the kitchen window, the light that shifted as his father raised his glass.

I can't live in this house any more, she began. *There is nothing
between your father and me any more. I love you very much. Don't you
ever doubt that. I want you to come and live with Harry and me when
we get settled.*

Allan had folded the letter and stuffed it in his pocket. He
walked down the yard and sat on the grass, in the depression.
He watched the trees in their wordless chorus, the way the
branches seemed to nod in agreement with some purpose he
could not understand. He lay back and looked at the stars and
they seemed as never before so far, far away and so cold.

And then he had felt that he must dig a hole where he lay
— just dig.

* * *

The weight of the earth made his shoulders ache. His lower
back cramped with the unaccustomed strain. He was down
about a foot all the way around, digging in a spiral out from
the centre. The smooth wood of the handle stuck at and stung
his palm where the blister had burst, but he relished the pains,
all of them, and tramped again to the middle of his hole to
start the spiral again.

Hunger and thirst gnawed at him as he worked. It was late
morning. He had had no breakfast. His appetite had grown
lately, but he fought it now because he would have to go to
the kitchen where his father stood and watched and drank.
He glanced toward the house as he heaved another shovelful
out of the hole.

He saw his father turn away, caught in the act. Or was there
something else? He refused to look, but he heard his father's
voice raised, the word "bitch", and the screen door slammed.
Footsteps came toward him through the grass and another
voice:

"Hello, Allan."

"Hello." He kept digging.

"I'm sorry I couldn't tell you I was going. Harry and me . . . we just decided it was the only way. We didn't want a fight with your father, so we . . . What are you doing?"

"What does it look like?"

"I brought you a present . . . Allan, please look at me."

"What for?"

"I brought you a present."

"Thanks." His shovel twisted as he heaved and the load spilled beside him.

"Your skin looks better," she said.

He stiffened.

Her footsteps scraped the grass, receding, then the gravel beside the house. He heard a car start in front of the house and he turned and saw the bag. A yellow bag, Sunrise Records, Eaton Centre. She had left the receipt, $12.99. Paid too much. The tape was Neil Young, *Comes a Time.*

He dropped the cassette back into the bag and stood listening to his own tape. How many times through? The trees at the end of the yard counted with him. The bag fell into the earth at his feet and he took up the shovel again. The dirt was loose where he had piled it and the hole filled quickly. The sod could be replaced another day.

DNA

J. A. Hamilton

When Dad first calls me it's the week after my sixteenth birthday. I'm just sorry it's me who picks up the phone. If Mom had, she could've told him I'd been dead for six years. She could've said I'd run away to Toronto.

"Pumpkin, is that you?" a voice I don't recognize says.

"Who is this?" I ask suspiciously. No one's called me Pumpkin in about a million years.

"Melanie?"

"Who wants to know?" This is a city, after all. It could be a creep. Some moron who calls up and breathes heavy and calls girls Pumpkin.

"Honey, it's your dad."

"My dad?" I say slowly. "You don't sound like Dad to me." My father — my stepfather, I should say — has a grumbly low voice, a bad cop's voice. This is definitely not him.

"Melanie, sweetheart, it's your real dad."

I honestly don't get it. I tell him, "I think you have the wrong number."

"Melanie, don't hang up. I'm him. The one your mother divorced."

I understand in a flash. My voice comes out high and screechy. "Dad?" I look around to see who might have over-heard.

"Hi, honey," he says. I can almost hear a smile in his voice, the relief. "Guess it's been too long."

Holy moley. My hands are shaking. My knees are knocking. Neither of us says anything for the longest time. I go through this rush of emotions in cartoon speed — awe, confusion, anger — and then shout into the silence, "Not long enough!" and slam down the phone. I lift my right hand up and watch it quiver. My father? My *real* father? He left when I turned five. I remember him taking me to the zoo on my birthday and telling me, in front of the polar bears, that he had to go away. I remember him saying he'd always love me. I waited for him. I really did. When we studied polar bears in grade two I held my breath till I turned blue and passed out. I waited for him until I was eleven, but he never came home. Not once.

I go up to my room and try to concentrate on my math homework. I hear my brother and mother come in, then my stepfather. Mom calls me down to set the table and while I'm putting the knives on the place mats she asks if anything interesting happened at school today.

"Only the moon fell out of the sky," I mumble. I expect her to know. I'm not going to tell her but I really think she ought to know anyway, like how when I was little she always knew when I stole candy.

But she's flipping hamburgers. She pushes a stray strand of hair out of her eyes and says, "What?"

"Nothing," I say. "School was copacetic."

"Good," she says.

"How was work?" I ask. I take the butter and salt and pepper to the table. Mom is a lawyer who does mostly legal aid work for poor women.

"All right," she says and nods wearily. I know she's probably thinking of a stubborn case, one her client won't win. "Your dad had some good luck, though," she adds.

Dad: what a tough word. This dad is an investigator for unsolved homicides. "About the genetic fingerprinting?"

"Let him tell you at supper," she says. "You'll be thrilled."

* * *

The genetic fingerprinting thing is really neat. Dad is so excited he can hardly eat. He says, "Pass the mustard," and then uncaps it and forgets to use it. Two forensic people have been accepted into a training program in Washington, he says.

What this means is the investigators will learn to type DNA from samples found at the scene of a crime (a murderer's stray hair, for instance), then, if the DNA exactly matches a suspect's, they've got their man. It means no one innocent can ever be jailed; no one guilty, once arrested, can go free. It's so precise it's amazing. I find all of it riveting. It really takes my mind off other things. Math homework, real fathers.

Then my geek brother says in this notice-me way: "I got a strange card today." He's real dramatic, dragging every word out, wiggling his eyebrows. He's almost fifteen and a genius with computers. Once he broke into the school's Macs and upped all his friends' grades. He got kicked out and now he buses to a high school across town. Other than with machines he's pretty nerdy.

"Pass the pickles," I say because I've got a sinking feeling in the pit of my stomach. If we genetic-coded my real dad and me, we'd match. I guess what Tim's going to say, that our real dad contacted him too, so I blurt out that I just tried marijuana.

"You what!" Mom says.

I grin. "Sorry, just kidding." I wink at Dad.

Of course Mom's apoplectic and frowning so hard her forehead looks like a ripple potato chip. "Melanie, for God's sake. Don't ever kid about something like that."

I've distracted her. The feeling in my stomach goes away a little bit. I've even distracted Tim. "Everyone smokes it," he says.

"That's not true, Tim," Mom says. Her mouth is pinched. Mom was a pothead way back and she's totally weird about drugs. She said she almost ruined her life with pot. "I know that's not true. Not these days."

"How would *you* know?" I ask Tim. No way does he smoke pot or even hang out with someone who does. He's too completely out of it.

"I know. Let's just say I know." Tim has a patch of tomato seeds on his chin and he's talking with his mouth full. Sometimes I want to disown him, send him somewhere else to be someone else's kid brother. I hear it's nice in Antarctica.

"You know how the topic of drugs upsets your mother," Dad says to me, that grizzly bear voice. "Why would you want to upset your mother?"

"Sorry," I say and shrug. "It just slipped out."

* * *

After I've excused myself I get up to look through the mail. There's nothing there for me so I breathe a sigh of relief.

But after school the next day when my friend Jody and I are on our way home, Jody bumps into me and elbows me. "Don't look now, Melanie, but someone's following us."

Of course I turn around and look. There's a man back there, a guy about forty with long hair. He stares right at me. Jody and I quicken our pace. So does he. We hear his footsteps behind us and start jogging, then running toward Jody's house. Fortunately, she only lives a couple blocks from school.

"Melanie!"

Jody keeps running but I stop dead. I know who it is.

Jody shouts. "Mel, come on!"

But I turn slowly around. There he is, this shabby looking guy with a beer gut, wheezing and holding his stomach.

"Wait up, Melanie," he says and stumbles closer.

"Mel," says Jody. She's yanking on my elbow. "Mel, let's get out of here."

"It's okay," I tell her. "I know who it is." I start walking backwards and shout at him, "What do you want?"

I let him get close. "Just talk to me, Melanie," he says. There's a thin layer of sweat all over his face. I see he looks a lot like Tim. Older, way older than Tim. Way messier too, since Tim's such a rabid neatness freak, but an amazing amount like him.

Then indecision clouds his face. "You are Melanie, right?"

"What business is it of yours?" I ask coolly. My books are heavy on my back and I scratch an ankle with my sneaker. Like I don't care.

He shakes his head. "You're beautiful."

I raise a shoulder and toss my hair back. "What's it to you?" Jody's pulling my elbow.

"I took your brother to lunch," he tells me. I notice how I like his eyes. I look in the mirror and wonder where I got mine, big, dark, and now there they are in his face. He's tall, I'm surprised how tall, probably six foot five. And thin, except for the beer gut.

But thinking all that makes me forget I hate him. I scrinch my eyes suspiciously. "That's a lie. Why would Tim go to lunch with you?"

"I'm his father," he explains with some exasperation. "Look, let's do something, whatever you want. Grab a milk-shake or something. I want to get to know you."

"Mom's a lawyer," I say. "Mom'll be mad about this."

"A lawyer?"

"My stepfather's a cop, so you better not try anything."

"You're my daughter."

Jody says, "Mister, get real." She yanks on my arm. "Come on, Melanie."

"I don't know you," I tell him. "Why should I go anywhere with you?"

He doesn't say anything. He just stares at me. Finally he touches my arm. Real lightly but it's like an electric shock. I jump back.

"No," he says, "let me look at you, I haven't seen you since . . . "

"Before I started school," I say. I'm rubbing my arm where he touched me. "Before I could tie my own shoelaces."

He smiles. He has uneven teeth and an overbite like mine before I had braces.

"Forget it," I say and turn and walk away.

"Please, Melanie?"

Jody says, "Just keep walking."

* * *

I don't know how to cope with seeing him. At Jody's house I call Dad and ask if I can come down to the precinct. I feel like I have jumping beans inside me.

"Something wrong?"

"No. Uh-uh. I just want to ask you something," I tell him. Like he can't see through me. Like he can't see through even vicious criminals, guys who maim small children, rapists. Who am I kidding?

"Grab a cab," he tells me. "I'll pay at this end."

"Thanks," I say, relieved. He'll know what to do.

At the station Dad meets my cab and takes me right away down to the lab. He sets up two microscopes side by side and gestures for me to look. I hop on a stool and look at the first and then the second.

"Are they the same?" Dad asks. "Does slide A match slide B? Do we or do we not have the killer?"

"You got him," I answer.

"Hypothetically. These are samples from Washington." He helps me down. "Six months from now we'll have that guy who's been doing those women downtown."

"Doing those women." Terms like that make me wild for my stepfather. He takes me into his office, then goes back out to get me a Coke. He knows something's up. I haven't hung out here after school since a year ago. I stopped when Jody moved to town and I started being more active in real things like her and boys and baseball. But he doesn't ask.

Finally I say, "You adopted us, right?" I burp from the fizz in my Coke. In public a burp would humiliate me. At the hamburger stand with senior guys around, a burp would mortify me.

Dad shrugs. "Sure, I adopted you."

"My father's in town. I mean my other dad, my real dad. See, he came to school today. And called the house last night. And I think Tim got a letter or something from him." There go those tears again, right on schedule.

Dad leans toward me but there's no other change. Just like a cop: I never know what he's thinking. Still, weirdly, he's easy to talk to, he never leaps down my throat like Mom is prone to do.

"I don't know what to do," I tell him, sniffling.

"What do you want to do?"

I shrug and wipe my nose on my shirt sleeve. "He looks like Tim."

"A lot," Dad says and nods. "I used to know him."

"You knew my father?"

"We went to high school together, played on the football team. He was quarterback. Then he got involved with your mother and they dropped out. She's told you that, about how they dropped out and joined a commune and had babies — and then he left her. It was too much for him, a wife and kids."

"Have you ever heard from him? Has Mom?"

Dad shakes his head. "Never."

"So why's he doing this?" I ask.

"Maybe he grew up." Dad stands and paces. "Have you told your mother?"

I shake my head. Dad's office is air-conditioned and I've got goose bumps. I hug myself. "I don't want to see him. I hate him for what he did."

"Running out on you."

"He said he'd come back. He promised." I can't help it, admitting this makes the tears come back. I used to take my real father's yearbook picture into my room and close the door and sit and stare at it when I needed to feel sorry for myself. Poor fatherless me. But I hadn't done that for years.

Dad moves to me and rubs my shoulder. "He didn't mean to hurt you, Mel."

I grab onto him. "He wasn't any good. He still isn't. He looks like a bum."

"It's okay if you want to see him."

"I don't want to see him," I say, sniffing. I consider. "Once, maybe."

"Do you want some help? Can I do anything?"

"I don't know. Yes. Come with me."

"You want me with you?" he asks. He passes me a Kleenex. I blow my nose and smile. I say weakly, "You're my dad."

* * *

At dinner it all comes out. Tim and I tell Mom about our real father. Tim has a lot more to say, like that he's a millionaire living in Vancouver.

I cough out my milk. "Ha!"

"He is. He's a surgeon in Vancouver. That's why he's in town, a convention or something. He's really rich."

Mom and Dad and I eye each other. Fourteen is just so *young*.

"You're going to see him, Melanie?"

"Sure," I say. "I guess. Why not?" A challenge.

"Do you know where to contact him, Tim?" Dad asks. "Did he tell you what hotel he's staying at?"

Tim nods.

"I'll call," I say, swallowing. "Let me."

It is a conversation of stutters. I don't know who is more uncomfortable, my real father or me. My neck gets hot and itchy as I get out that Tim and I will meet him at Lulu's, a Mexican food place halfway between our schools. At six on Friday? We agree. I hang up and tell Tim. Dad says he'll come for moral support.

I'm so overwrought I can't sleep. I toss and turn and tangle my sheets. I hear Mom and Dad coming up to bed after one. They start to argue. I pull a pillow over my head because I don't want to know about it. I have memories of Mom and my real dad fighting and though my new dad hardly ever raises his voice, it sends shivers through me when he does. I wouldn't want to be a murderer.

But I can't help overhearing some of it. Mom isn't mad at Dad. She's mad at my real dad. I wouldn't want to be him, either. I feel sorry for him.

The next day at school I keep expecting to see him. I've got Jody watching too, all through baseball practice, even though she thinks it's retarded for me to want to see him again. I take a ball on my thumb because I'm not concentrating. It swells up and turns purple and I sit the rest of the practice out on the bleachers.

It's surprising how I watch for him on the way home. I even look behind bushes. Yup. A real, regular sixteen-year-old, looking for her father behind shrubs. I must be nuts.

At home every noise sends me rushing for the door. Every time the phone rings I have it in a second.

Then when Tim gets home I corral him. "Well?" I make him show me the card our real father sent him. It's a card for about a five-year-old, with a little boy in a cowboy hat on the front cover. *Thinking of you*, it says, *Love, Dad.* It makes me jealous.

"I don't remember him," Tim tells me. "He looks like me and everything, but I don't remember a single thing about him."

"Me either, hardly," I say. "Sort of I do but not really. And you were only three when he left." I start making cheese on crackers, watching out for the thumb. I'll probably lose my fingernail; it's black and blue. "Want some?"

"Sure," he says, grabbing the plate.

I grab it back. We sit at the table, eating. "Dad's my dad," Tim says through this gross mouthful of crackers and cheddar. "I don't even know this guy."

"Don't talk with your mouth full," I say. I nibble a cracker and sigh.

"I told him about my computer stuff and he didn't even care. All he wanted was to talk about himself."

"So all you ever want," I tell him, "is to talk about yourself."

"Very funny, Mirabelle," Tim says. I stick out my tongue at the nickname.

* * *

Dad gives me money, and Thursday Jody and I go to the mall to buy me a new outfit. In the store mirror, wearing it, I look cool, I look good. From a distance. Really my nails are bitten to the quick and my hair's frizzy and I'm as nervous as if Jody's big brother, her college brother, just asked me out.

But I hope it isn't obvious. At Lulu's Tim and I share a booth underneath a hanging piñata and Dad sits across the room drinking coffee, to be there, he says, if we need him. I calmly order a New York Seltzer and Tim gets a Pepsi.

But we can't drag our eyes from the door.

"What if he doesn't come?" Tim says, twisting in his seat.

"He'll come, Tim. He's five minutes late is all."

We wait. I order refills and . . . "Do you think he likes nachos?"

Tim says, "Everyone likes nachos."

"Nachos," I say firmly. "A double order."

At seven Tim gets up and pushes the door open, peers along the street. Nothing.

"He's coming," I tell Dad angrily when I see him crossing over. "He'll be here."

But he isn't. I get more and more mortified, more and more mad. When I was little, I thought he left because I was bad.

Finally, at 7:20, the waitress brings a message. "Are you Melanie Ackerman?"

"What? What is it?"

"Your father called to cancel." She looks down at a slip of paper. "He says, 'I had second thoughts.' " She looks back up at me.

I grab the note and skim it. I wad it, throw it at Tim and jerk up. I find the pay phone and call his hotel. When they say he's checked out I bang the receiver against the phone. Before I know it I take off running. I run and run and run, seeing nothing, sobbing and yelling. One of my new sandals falls off and, cursing, I rip the other one free and throw it as hard as I can at the window of a butcher shop. Then I sag to the pavement, pounding it with my fists.

* * *

After that a calm descends me. I walk around for the next two weeks in a total haze. I get a B on a physics test I can't even remember taking. My thumb turns black, then green and finally the bruise fades almost totally. I keep my nail. It goes bumpy but Mom says she's sure it won't fall off.

I ask her how I can love someone who doesn't deserve to be loved. I've been thinking a lot about this because I kind of think I should love him. I ask Mom if it's okay to love him since I have this automatic thing that it's only okay to love one dad at a time. Otherwise it feels like I'm, I don't know, two-timing. It's taken a whole bunch of courage to even ask such a stupid question and I've waited until we're in the grocery store, her and me alone. I make like I'm pricing different brands of frozen orange juice and say it real quick in a sort of a mumble: "I used to really love him." Then I add bravely, "Maybe I still do."

"Take the Old South," Mom says. "Six cans."

I put them in the buggy, and when we walk up past the TV dinners Mom clears her throat. "I still have a lot of resentment. Your father brought out a part of me I didn't much like, you know."

"That was a long time ago, Mom." As if I'm a paragon of forgiveness.

"Yeah," she agrees, "and also it's my resentment, not yours. I need to remember that." She stops and turns to me.

"I'm ashamed of him," I tell her.

Mom nods. "But he has his good points, I suppose. He must. He is your father, Melanie. He chose your name. He always will be your father and nothing can change that."

I stare at her a minute and walk away. She lets me. I go to the aisle with cookies and stare at the marshmallow ones. I can't eat chocolate or my face breaks out. My brother can eat about twenty-two bags. I think, my father named me Melanie. I keep thinking that: my father chose my name. Mom's right. Even if he's an unreliable zero and I never see him again, I can love him if I want. I can love him and still be mad he left. This makes me feel immensely, suddenly, relieved. I grab three bags of cookies. Then a fourth.

The next day Tim and I get a greeting card from Mexico. The front cover is of a semi-nude dancer and inside it says, "Wish you were here." Some Mexican money falls out.

Tim blinks and says, "He's no millionaire in Vancouver."

I smile. "First base," I say.

Tim thinks for a minute. He picks up a peso and turns it over in his hand. "He's not anything a father's supposed to be."

"Second base," I say.

"He's not going to call us," Tim says, grinning and getting into the spirit of it.

"Third base, Tim." Tim wouldn't know a base if he tripped over it.

"But he's ours?" Tim asks.

"Home run," I say and slap him in the head.

* * *

At dinner Tim asks if we can adopt Dad. Dad raises his eyebrows.

"Can we, Mom? Is it legal? I mean, Dad, you adopted us. But we never adopted you. Right?"

Maybe Tim has half a brain after all.

"Great plan," I tell him.

Even Mom nods. "I like it."

"It would be an honour," Dad says solemnly, "to be adopted by you two."

That's just what we do. Mom draws up some papers and Tim and I adopt Dad. Then we go to Dad's office, all four of us, and watch a forensic scientist from Washington isolate a DNA. Genetic fingerprinting.

"That's the guy you just adopted," the woman says, showing us. I wait while Tim looks in. Then I have a turn. Rows of black marks like x-rays rise towards me. I wonder if it really is Dad's DNA — probably not, I figure. It's probably just for show.

"And here's yours and Tim's," the scientist says, winking to let us in on their game, gesturing to two scopes down the bench.

Even though nobody took hair samples from either of us, Tim and I peer in. The same black dots materialize.

"Well," asks Dad, "do they match?"

I kiss his cheek. He hugs us, Tim on one side, me on the other, while Mom cocks her head at us.

Inside I raise a toast to my real father, knowing there's a place in me that's all his, that belongs only to him. I'm sad, sure, and still a bit lonely. But I smile up at Dad. It's cute, what he and the scientist have done, making our DNA match. I say, "Oh yeah. Absolutely. We've got our man."

Sugar Train

Wayne Arthurson

O ne hundred miles this way," he says, pointing to the east. "And two hundred miles that way," he says, pointing to the west with his other hand. "The longest stretch of straight track in the world. No track longer and straighter."

"That's not true," she says. "You're making that up."

"It is true," he says, waving his arms to the pale blue sky.

"Is not."

"Is too. I read it, and since I did, it's true."

"Where'd you read it?" she asked.

"In a book."

"What book?

"One of the big, red ones on the third shelf."

"A big, red one?"

"With the small words and the little pictures."

"I can't read those books," she declared.

"Of course not," he said. "You're too small."

"No, I'm not. The words in the book are too small."

"So are you."

"Am not."

The boy ignores her remaining words and slowly walks down the track. Straight it goes, into the desert. Straight into the red-brown rock. Straight to where the colour green refuses to exist naturally, only the red-brown of the rocks and sand. Even the vegetation is brown, burnt dry by the white heat of the sun. Red-brown the only colour to the horizon.

The girl pauses and sees the boy walking down the track away from her. She runs to catch up, jumping slightly so every step will land on a railway tie. "Wait for me . . . wait for me!"

They follow the track towards the buildings; three identical government designed houses, huddled together thirty metres south of the railway track. Thirty metres south of the houses, a highway runs parallel to the track, stretching east and west as far as it can in a straight line. Along the railway track, a wooden platform stands on its six, metre-high legs made out of discarded railway ties. The boy takes three quick steps and leaps onto the platform. He sits down facing the track, his feet swinging over the edge. The girl moves up the platform and squints up at the boy. She stares at him for several seconds and then moves around the platform. She climbs the stairs and comes up behind the boy. She sits next to him and her feet also swing over the edge.

"When?" the girl asks. The boy doesn't answer, so she asks again. "When?"

"When? When what?"

"When will he come?" she asks.

"Oh. Him. He'll be here next week."

"How long is that?"

"Seven days. Seven times the sun goes up and down, and he'll show up. First Thursday in December is in seven days."

"I know seven days," the girl says, showing five fingers on one hand and the thumb and index on the other. "One, two, three, four, five, six, seven."

"First Thursday in December," he says.

"Seven days," she says.

"Seven days," he repeats.

"What if he doesn't come?" she asks.

The boy looks down at the girl as if she just spit in his face. "He'll come. He always comes on the first Thursday in December. You know that. You saw him last year."

"That's right. I did see him last year."

The boy nods. "And you remember what he came on?"

The girl smiles at her brother and he smiles back. Simultaneously they say: "The Sugar Train. Santa Claus always comes on the Sugar Train."

* * *

The screen door slams behind the girl as she enters the middle house. "Is Santa coming this year again?" she asks her mother.

The woman is tall and thin with long, straight hair reaching the small of her back. She wears a pale brown skirt, and a simple white T-shirt covers her torso. Her face is attractive — a long thin nose over a slightly pouting mouth — and her eyes are blue. Black half moons hang underneath her eyes. Her skin is tight and dry, ravaged by the wind, sun, and heat of the desert. She has her hands dipped into a tubful of soapy water. The girl walks up to her mother and yanks on the skirt. Her mother looks down and smiles. "Is Santa coming on the Sugar Train again?" The girl asks. The smile disappears. "He's supposed to, Manda, but I don't know yet."

"Why not?"

"I don't know."

"Why not? Doesn't he want to come?"

The woman turns away from the tub and kneels down to her daughter. The girl is almost a tiny mirror image of her mother: tall and thin for her age, with long, dirty-blonde hair; dirty-blonde due to the sand and wind, not natural colouring. The woman sighs and brushes a few hairs from her daughter's face. "Santa might come, Manda. We'll just have to wait and see."

"Till next week," Manda says with a smile.

"Next week," her mother replies, returning the smile.

"That's seven days," Manda says and shows her hands, counting each finger. "One, two, three, four, five, six, seven."

"That's wonderful, Manda. But you counted twenty-five last week, didn't you?"

"Now I can do fifty. Henry showed me how."

"Good for him. Where is Henry?"

Manda points to the door. "Outside. Waiting for the Sugar Train."

The woman stands up and returns to her dishes. "Tell him to come in. Dinner will be ready soon." Manda turns and begins to run to the door. "Manda!" her mother shouts. Manda stops. "Don't run," her mother says. Manda sheepishly drops her head and slowly walks to the door. She pushes it open, looks back at her mother and then rushes outside. "Henry! Henry!" she shouts. "Dinner's ready!"

Later, the family gathers round the dining room table, eating. The meal is sparse: a few potatoes, one or two thin slices of meat, and a small leaf of lettuce for each person.

"I don't like this food," Henry says.

His mother replies without looking up from her plate. "Eat your food, Henry."

"But I don't like it."

"Of course you do. You ate it yesterday."

"That's why I don't like it. We had this yesterday. And the day before. Why can't we have anything else?"

His mother straightens in her chair and looks at him. "Because there isn't anything else."

"Is it because of the strike?" Henry asks.

The mother is briefly startled. She looks at her husband on the opposite side of the table, but his head is down and he eats his meal, oblivious to the conversation. She looks back at Henry. "Who told you about that?"

"I read it in the newspaper."

"Where'd you read the newspaper?"

"In Dad's chair. There's a strike, right? It said so in the paper."

The woman opens her mouth to speak, but a slow rumbling stops her. The rumbling starts softly, glasses and china tinkling as if a small tremor is passing through. Then, as the shaking becomes more intense, the table and chairs vibrate heavily. The shaking continues to increase with intensity until the entire house and its contents are shaking. Dust rises from the floor and falls off the walls and ceiling. Each member of the family calmly leans over their plate to protect the food from the dust. Soon, the sound of diesel engines is heard, and the heavy roar of truck-trains racing along the highway fills the house with noise. Headlights glare into the room showing one, two, three, four and finally, five truck-trains racing by. The noise and vibrations follow the trucks and slowly begin to subside until only the china and glasses tinkle.

"What's a strike?" Manda asks when the silence returns.

"Not now, Manda," says her mother. "Eat your dinner. You too, Henry."

The boy sits back in his chair and pushes his plate forward. "I don't want to eat."

"Henry!" his mother says.

"What's a strike?" Manda asks again. "Is it bad?"

"It's very bad," Henry says to her. "I read about it in the newspaper."

"I can't read the newspaper. Yet."

"Well, I can and it says there's a strike in the Port and it's bad because the Sugar Train . . . "

"Henry!" The father speaks and the boy stiffens at the sound. Like the rest of his family, the father's skin is tight and dry. His hair is short-cropped and his nose is slightly out of line. He squints even though the light is dim. His thin lips cover yellow teeth, some now turning black with decay. "Stop being a pest," he says to Henry. "Eat your food."

The boy obeys immediately, leaning forward and slowly putting a piece of potato in his mouth. Manda watches him, smiling to herself. "You too, Amanda. Eat your dinner." Manda's smile disappears and she turns back to her food. While the children eat, the adults look across the table at each other. Her right eyebrow rises and he shrugs in response. Shaking his head. Shaking his head.

* * *

The next day, the sun rises over the desert; jagged stones, square buildings, bare bushes cast long shadows over the plain.

The truck is blue, but like everything else, covered by a thin layer of red-brown dust. There are spots of rust on the body and cracks in all the windows. The truck has more than a metre's clearance and although all four tires are fully inflated, the treads are well-worn. A rusted grill-guard hangs off the front and a spare tire holder hangs empty off the back.

It takes one battery charger charging through the night, a pint of diesel poured straight into the carb, a piece of wood shoved into the choke and fifteen minutes of trying to turn the engine before the truck explodes to life, first spewing a cloud of black smoke and then a continuous stream of blue. The engine rumbles in only four of its eight cylinders with a fifth and sixth kicking in now and then.

He turns on the wipers to smear the dust across the windshield and allows the truck to idle loudly for 10 minutes. Finally, he grinds the truck into gear and pulls out, trailing dust behind him. The truck begins to shudder as he increases speed, but it steadies somewhat near eighty klicks.

He looks back, but only for a few seconds.

* * *

Later that same day, Henry is holding half a peanut butter sandwich in his left hand and a glass of milk in his other. He is sitting at the table and his mother is sitting opposite him.

"Where's Dad?" Henry asks while chewing.

"Don't talk with your mouth full," she says.

"Sorry," he says and then swallows. "Where's Dad?"

"He went to Port Augusta."

"Did he take the truck?" he asks and she nods. "I thought so. I heard something this morning, but I thought it was a dream. Guess it wasn't."

She sighs. "No, you weren't dreaming. Dad took the truck."

"What for?"

"You said so last night. There's a strike on and the trains aren't running. The Sugar Train's not coming so we're running out of food."

Henry stops in mid-bite, quickly pulling the sandwich away. "We're outta food?"

His mother smiles and reaches across the table to tousle his hair. "No, we're not out of food. We're just running low. Dad went to Port Augusta to get some."

"So we can still eat?"

"We can still eat. Just get used to potatoes for a little while without complaining about it, okay?"

He swallows the rest of the sandwich and then downs the glass of milk. "Yeah, okay," he says. He looks up and meets her gaze. "Can I go?"

"You can go," she says, laughing softly. "Go play with your sister outside." Henry stands up and saunters to the door. He pulls the screen door open but his mother yells after him. "Don't say anything about the strike and the Sugar Train to your sister — okay, Henry?"

Henry looks at his mother and then outside. He pauses and then looks back at his mother. "It's not coming, is it, Mom?"

She shakes her head. "Probably not."

"She's going to miss Santa Claus, you know. I've been telling her he's supposed to come next week."

"Then stop it. Don't get her hopes up."

"She'll ask."

"I know, but try not to get her hopes up too much."

"I'll try," he says and then he steps outside, allowing the screen door to slam behind him.

Amanda is sitting on the platform facing the track, swinging her legs back and forth. She hears the screen door slam and sees her brother leaving the house. She waves to him. "Henry! Over here!" Henry doesn't look up, so she shouts louder to attract his attention. "Over here! Henry! Over here!" Henry looks up, squinting in the bright daylight. He waves at her. She waves back. "Over here!" she shouts again.

Henry shuffles over to the platform, kicking a few rocks along the way. He doesn't climb the platform but walks around the front to stand in front of his sister. "Hi," she says, smiling brightly.

He nods once and peers down the track.

"Did Dad leave?" she asks. He nods again. "Where'd he go?"

It takes several seconds before Henry answers. "He went
to Port Augusta."

"Why?"

"Because."

"Because why?"

"He had to pick up some stuff."

"What stuff?"

He snaps at her. "I don't know. He didn't tell me, Mom
didn't tell me, so I don't know, okay?"

Amanda's bright smile disappears and her head drops.
Her feet stop swinging. Henry looks at his sister, at the track,
at his sister and then back to the track. He takes a quick deep
breath and begins to walk away from the platform. Amanda
remains seated on the platform, her head down. Henry walks
about twenty metres and then, without turning back, yells to
his sister: "Come on, Manda! Let's go!"

Manda sits up quickly and jumps off the platform. She
runs toward her brother, jumping slightly so she can land
each step on a railway tie. "Wait for me!" she shouts. "Wait
for me!"

The two walk away from the platform, he balancing on
one rail and she jumping from railway tie to railway tie.
Finally she asks him. "Six days, right?"

"What?"

"Six days. Santa Claus comes in six days, right?"

"You bet," he says. "I don't care what they say, Santa Claus
always comes on the first Thursday in December. He always
comes on the Sugar Train."

Manda jumps and misses a railway tie. She quickly jumps
back on. "That's six days, right?"

"You bet, Manda. Santa Claus comes on the Sugar Train
in six days."

"I know six," she says, holding up her hands, showing all fingers on one and just the thumb on the other. "One, two, three, four, five, six."

The Visitor

Christine Pinsent-Johnson

I was getting fed up with saying goodbye. One month five kids disappeared from my shrinking class at Copelin High School. At this rate, there would be a class of one graduating next year, and that one would be me.

I was witnessing the slow death of a town and there was nothing I or anyone else could do about it. All over the world people unite to fight for something they believe in, like preserving an old-growth forest or protecting the ozone. But no one bothered to fight for Copelin. My dad claimed people had simply accepted their fate; they knew the mines wouldn't last forever and now they realized it was time to move on.

Last night I overheard my parents talking about moving to St. John's or the mainland. At least my mom was talking; Dad was trying to avoid the discussion.

"The Greenes are leaving next month," Mom said casually while stirring the spaghetti sauce. "Frank got a job in Grand Falls at the mill."

I knew Mom wanted to leave as much as I did. The fridge was cluttered with want ads from the St. John's, Halifax, and Toronto newspapers.

"I guess we'll have to find someone else to play cards with," Dad said. His attempt to avoid the discussion.

"That's not the point. We're losing two more good friends." Mom stopped stirring and started rubbing her neck, which stiffened whenever she was upset. "This is really getting ridiculous," she said quietly. "Why don't you start looking ... "

"We've already been through this, Joanne. I won't be able to find anything better than what I have."

Dad was sitting across the table from me. I kept staring at my biology textbook, hoping they would keep me out of it.

"I'm committed to stay here at least another couple of years," Dad said as he walked over to Mom. He gently placed her hands at her side and began massaging her neck. "You know I wouldn't be able to find anything better."

Dad was one of the last people to work for the Copelin Mining and Refining Company, which had built the town over sixty years ago. He was the property manager for all the residential buildings, and spent his days running after people for overdue rent and closing up empty houses. About once every couple of months he actually sold a house. Usually it was to one of the retired miners and his wife, determined to stay here until they died.

But most of his days were spent knocking on doors, trying to convince unemployed miners and millworkers to pay months of back rent. Last winter he had to change the locks on two families, forcing them out of their homes. One family quickly left Copelin but the other ended up living with their relatives in the trailer park near the highway. They still won't talk to my dad. He never changed any more locks after that.

I had to leave. I couldn't stand another non-discussion about leaving Copelin.

"Where are you going?" Mom asked, when she saw me get up from the kitchen table. "Supper will be ready in half an hour."

"I'm going out. I'll be back in a few minutes."

"Do you think it's a good idea to go out just before supper?" Dad asked, clearing his throat nervously.

Why can't he just say "Don't go out" or "Be back before supper," I thought. "I won't be long," I said, closing the textbook.

"Well, William, you said that the other day. Heh hemmm. And you were late for supper." I hated it when he used my full name. It sounded so fake. As if he was trying too hard.

"I'll be back before supper," I snapped, getting even more irritated. I could feel the sweat beading on my forehead in the steamy kitchen. The window beside the stove was dripping with condensation. I had to get out of there.

"Don't use that tone with your father," said Mom sharply.

Why does she have to stick up for him? Why can't he just say I'm being a brat and get it over with? I couldn't even look at him. I kept staring at the moisture droplets racing down the window.

"As long as you say you'll be back, I guess you can go."

"Gee, thanks Dad." I knew I was being a jerk but I couldn't help it.

As I grabbed my coat off the living room chair I heard Mom say, "You know, you really shouldn't let him talk to you like that." Unbelievable.

The night air was overwhelmed by the sharp, almost suffocating smell of pine smoke from people's wood stoves. It had been raining the past few days, and there was a hazy mixture of fog and wood smoke hanging over the town.

Most of the snow had washed away except for some skeletal remains along the edges of the street and in the ditches. Everyone kept saying they were lucky it was such a mild winter because there was no money for snowplowing. But now the potholes needed to be filled, and there was no money for that either.

Out of a dozen homes on the street five were empty. At the Purdys' house the front door was wide open, leaving the house exposed. I could look straight into the empty living room, where Mrs. Purdy used to sit and wait for her daughter, Michelle, after I walked her home from the dances at the stadium last summer. I ran up the front steps and quickly shut the door.

I turned onto Main Street, walked past the empty lot where the theatre used to be. It had burnt down along with the bowling alley and company store ten years ago. The company only rebuilt the store. They'd stopped showing movies at the theatre anyway, and said it was too expensive to rebuild the bowling alley. The only thing left besides the company store was the bank, post office, and Reid's Bakery, which didn't sell sweets any more, just bread and rolls.

Four streets ran perpendicular to Main. Three of these streets were filled with row houses, three units to a row, three bedrooms in a home. They were neat, orderly army-style homes, low on looks and high on efficiency. No grass in the yards, only rocks and weeds. Almost every home had a clothes-line, cutting across the back yard, supported by a cedar rail in the middle. The fourth street, which was ours, was a combination of row homes and small single houses that looked just like row houses, except for the metre gap in between. The bigger single homes were uptown, closer to the mine offices. They were for the geologists, engineers, and office employees. The miners with families lived downtown, and the men from around the bay lived in the bunk houses on the outskirts of town.

I should have been born twenty years ago when the mines were still running and the company took care of everything. There was no other place like Copelin in all of Newfoundland. For a small town, about 3,000 at its peak, Copelin had everything you'd find in a city like St. John's or Corner Brook. There was a movie theatre, restaurant, bowling alley, shooting range, swimming pool, playing fields, and a stadium. For years, Copelin had one of the best hockey teams on the island. The company would even pay for train tickets so fans could cheer on the team during road games. Now there wasn't even a hockey team. It wasn't fair.

* * *

In early spring Spruce first wandered into town. He was seen ambling silently down Main Street, stooping occasionally to munch the dandelions growing beside the road, as if he were doing nothing out of the ordinary. Mrs. Tilley saw him first, although she didn't know what she saw at the time. I heard her in the post office talking to a group of women.

"My dears, you're not going to believe what I saw last night," she said breathlessly. "I was out for my walk and when I rounded the corner of Ore Street I stared straight into the glaring red eyes of the devil itself."

The women in the post office passed knowing glances to each other and smiled politely. Mrs. Tilley was known for spending long nights at the union hall and staggering home just before her husband woke up.

"You must have been frightened," said the postmaster, from behind the counter.

Mrs. Tilley didn't seem to notice his mocking tone. "My dears, I nearly jumped out of me skin. Them eyes was some creepy, and he didn't even move. I just backed up slow so I wouldn't startle him. Then I high-tailed it home."

At first everyone thought Mrs. Tilley had had one too many until Reverend Sharpe saw Spruce a couple of days later. The devil which appeared in front of Mrs. Tilley was actually a young bull moose. This time, he was spotted downtown, sniffing around the trash bins behind the company store.

Then later that same morning, Daisy Miller said she saw Spruce in the empty lot beside the bank, where the theatre once stood. He was again nuzzling through the trash cans.

After the first sightings people began to see Spruce a couple of times a week. It was Daisy Miller who started calling him Spruce. Ten years ago her Uncle Spruce and a few other men rescued a moose that had fallen through the ice on Beothuk Lake. It was Spruce Miller who crawled across the ice to lasso the semi-conscious moose, which they tied to a bull-dozer from one of the mines, and hauled out.

I first saw Spruce a few days later. He began to get a little bolder and wandered into town during the late afternoons. He usually came out of the bush at the north end of town around three o'clock, as if he was waiting for a polite time to come calling.

I was struggling with the last question on a math test. Looking out the classroom window for some divine inspiration, I saw Spruce strolling through the school yard. I watched him in silence, hoping no one else would notice him. There were only five other students in my grade ten class. Ever since I was in grade six the school board had been threatening to close the school and bus everyone into the nearest town, an hour's drive up the highway.

Spruce was taking his time, obviously having no destination in mind. He was a picture of contradictions. His long spindly legs looked like they would break under his round bulk of a body. His soft brown eyes were overwhelmed by a massive snout which ended with a flapping upper lip, and his ears looked too small for his long, narrow face. His antlers were just beginning to grow and were covered with a velvety soft fuzz. I was surprised to see how gracefully he moved. I always thought moose were awkward-looking and clumsy, with their long, homely faces and humped backs.

I'd seen a couple of moose before, slung over the hood of a car after being hit on the highway or in the back of a pickup after hunting. My father was probably the only man in Copelin who didn't hunt, so I'd never seen a moose in the wild.

Just that morning, I'd overheard Albert Smith talking to Amanda Higgins, the bank teller, about the moose's lack of intelligence.

"He must be some stunned to come wandering into a town full of hunters," said Mr. Smith on the steps of the company store. "Don't he realize people here live all winter on a freezer full of his distant relatives?"

Amanda Higgins' double chin shook in agreement, "Maybe he's one of them backward moose. Maybe he's brain-injured."

"He'll be brain-injured if he don't quit eating my flowers. Sure, last week I found all my tulips stripped bare. I woulda' got my shotgun and killed him right then and there if I'd caught him."

Amanda Higgins' chins jiggled with excitement. They looked like the dewlap under Spruce's chin. "Yes bye. I knows I'd be hollerin' after him if I caught him in my garden. The animal's got no sense. No sense at all."

But not everyone thought Spruce was a nuisance. People began to set out treats for him, including my father. Rumour was he ate all the Purity Lemon Creams but left the carrots. Every time a sighting was made, Dad would run into the kitchen, grab a handful of biscuits and a couple of apples and set them on the back porch. One night I heard him walking around the back yard just after 2 a.m. He was calling out to the night, "Come on Spruce my son. I've got your favourites here."

I don't know if Spruce ever came that night. Dad was still out there when I fell asleep and neither of us said anything the next morning.

* * *

When I walked in the door after playing road hockey in front of Dave Rideout's place, the first thing I heard was the booming voice of Reverend Sharpe. He and Dave's father were having a cup of coffee with Dad in the kitchen. The two of them were on the town council; Mr. Rideout was the mayor and the Reverend was a councillor.

"He's getting to be a nuisance," said Reverend Sharpe. "Last week he dug up three flower gardens, eating up people's hard work and enjoyment."

"I heard he's been dragging people's trash all over their yards," said the mayor. "What happens if he ever gets aggressive and goes after one of the kids? You know kids. A little harmless teasing and in a second they could have a two-ton moose chasing after them."

"Sure, I heard Fanny Reid nearly ran into him as she rounded the corner of Main Street in her car the other evening. There he was standing in the middle of the road, refusing to budge," said the Reverend.

"It's our responsibility to do something before someone gets hurt," added the mayor. He was looking straight at my father, waiting for his input. The mayor often stopped by to discuss council issues with my dad. I guess my dad had a certain status in the town as one of the last company employees. Dad also gave the mayor an ego boost, since he would never disagree with him.

My father remained silent. I could see him swallowing, his Adam's apple bulging, as he prepared to clear his throat. But he didn't say anything. He didn't always agree with everything

the mayor and Reverend did on council, like the decision to
stop subsidizing the summer baseball league, but he went
along with them anyway.

Come on, say something, I silently urged from the hall. I
knew he disagreed with them. He'd set out at least two bags of
apples and three packages of biscuits since Spruce started
visiting regularly. I could feel myself turn red when I heard
him clear his throat. I slowly backed down the hall and went
upstairs to my room.

*　*　*

The mayor called a town meeting to discuss Spruce. Once
people found out that the mayor was thinking about getting
rid of the moose they began to take sides. It was all they could
talk about for a week. Petitions were sent around and signs
were posted in front yards and along fences, some saying *Let
Him Be* and others saying *He's Got To Go.* I'd never seen people
get so worked up over something. No one protested this much
when the mines closed.

The council meeting was moved from the municipal office,
a small room in the basement of the library, to the union hall
so everyone could attend. There was a reporter from the St.
John's newspaper, which never before bothered with small
town council meetings. The reporter wasn't much older than
me. He didn't even try to hide his boredom, just yawned and
doodled in his steno book.

The moose issue was shuffled to the bottom of the evening's agenda. I think the mayor hoped people would get
bored and leave the meeting before it ended. His nerves were
frazzled, speaking in front of so many people, and he kept
shuffling the papers in front of him. He'd never seen so many
bodies at a council meeting. The only people who usually

attended the meetings were a couple of old-timers with nothing better to do and the editor of the town paper.

My father asked me to go to the meeting with him. He said it was an important issue for the town, and it went beyond a simple decision to let Spruce stay or to force him out. I agreed to go partly because I was feeling guilty for the way I had been treating him the past few weeks.

After passing motions to recruit another volunteer firefighter, start collecting a dog tax, and approve a letter requesting the donation of library books, they finally reached the end of the agenda. A group of men, followed by a haze of their own cigarette smoke, stepped into the stifling hall, and everyone else stopped shuffling and whispering.

The discussion about Spruce started off respectfully enough. Representatives from both sides of the issue carefully stated their case as we sat in silence. My father looked over at me once, and started to smile but changed his mind and looked down at a piece of folded up paper he was holding.

The mayor, in an attempt at a compromise, asked the audience, "Why don't we get one of them tranquillizer guns, knock him out and let him go somewhere one hundred kilometres from here?"

A man in the back stood up. I'd seen him before, standing outside the Legion every afternoon, waiting for it to open. "We're some stunned to be sitting here arguing about this moose. Why don't we just kill it and get a nice bunch of steaks out of him."

"Yes, bye, we do that and we'll have them peace freaks and animal rights activists accusing us of cruelty to animals," said a woman from the middle of the crowd.

"What harm is he doing to ye. I say we just let him do his thing and leave him alone. It's the proper thing," said Mrs. Tilley. Her husband sat beside her shaking his head.

Then one of the old-timers jumped up and yelled, "Kill him before he tramples some poor child." Someone else in the back yelled, "Let the poor thing alone."

The St. John's reporter jerked his head up and began writing madly. Then everyone got into it. People were yelling back and forth at each other. The mayor kept banging his gavel on the table, but everyone ignored him. The reporter stopped his frantic writing for an instant to take a picture of the mayor yelling at everyone to shut up.

In the middle of the yelling and screaming my father stood up slowly. He never said a word in any sort of public meeting. I wanted to slip into the cracks of the floor and disappear. He unfolded his piece of paper and looked at it quickly. Then he folded it back up and held it tightly in his hand. The people around us stopped talking and looked at my father. Like a wave, silence gradually fell over the rest of the hall. He just stood there, waiting, gripping on to that piece of paper as if it gave him the strength to stand.

He quietly cleared his throat. His first words didn't quite make it out. Someone yelled, "Speak up, we can't hear you." He stopped. I thought he'd pack it in right there. But he didn't. He looked over at me. I couldn't help it, but I turned my eyes away and stared at my shoes.

He began again, a little louder this time, "Spruce has done something for this town that no one has seen for years."

"Yeah, he's picked up the garbage regularly," some wise-cracker yelled out."

"Uh, that's not my point," said Dad quietly. He started to unfold his paper and look at his notes. He was totally thrown off.

"Tell them about the treats," I whispered. "Tell them about all the times you and other people set out treats for Spruce, like it was Christmas or something." Dad looked down at me, nodded his head slightly and smiled. Then he released his grip on the paper and let it fall to the floor. I thought he had dropped it and when I bent down to pick it up he whispered, "Leave it there."

He began again. This time his voice was loud enough the first time. "How many of us have run into our kitchens to find special treats for Spruce every time he was spotted in town? When is the last time you felt that same excitement about something?"

I looked up at him, hoping he would see that I was listening to every word.

"Spruce has given us all a little hope, something almost magical, during a time when we don't have much of anything that's good." A few people in front of us were nodding in agreement. "I think it would be a foolish idea to get rid of him. I think we should just let him be." Dad didn't waste any time sitting down. People were still looking at him but he didn't acknowledge their stares.

I could tell people were stunned. No one said a word for a few seconds. The mayor screwed up his face as if he had a bad taste in his mouth. The reverend shrugged his shoulders and sighed. Once people digested everything an excited buzz spread throughout the union hall. I caught bits and pieces of the conversations around us.

"Maybe he's got a point."

"I can't believe Graham Percy stood up and . . . "

"But what if Spruce . . . "

"I've never heard him say that much at one time."

People were talking as much about my dad as they were about Spruce, but I didn't care. I reached down and picked up the crumpled paper my Dad had dropped and put it in my pocket.

"Thanks for your help, Willy," he said.

"You would have done fine without me. People really listened to what you had to say." I looked straight at him. For the first time I noticed the flecks of gold in his deep brown eyes. I had those same flecks.

"You think so?" He really didn't know. It was like he was a kid looking for someone to say he did the right thing.

"I know so," I said.

* * *

A week later council passed a special by-law protecting Spruce, and he was allowed to wander throughout the town freely. The newspaper article from the St. John's reporter ended up being reprinted in the *Globe and Mail.* Then early in June a CBC crew from St. John's did a piece about Spruce and troubled times for Copelin. Our forgotten town ended up being on the national news with the help of Spruce!

That summer my dad and a couple of other people, including the mayor, formed the C.C.C., the Citizens' Coalition for Copelin. They helped people get low-interest loans from the government so they could afford to buy their homes. People began painting their houses again, the sidewalks were fixed, and some of the potholes were repaired. Copelin would never be the same as it once was, but at least it wouldn't become a forgotten ghost town, and maybe I wouldn't be the only one left by the time I graduated from high school.

Bridges

S. E. Lee

What was a staircase like that doing in an old folks' home, I wanted to know! It reminded me of the one at school, all slippery surface and sharp edges. Staircases like those weren't made for old people. For the amount of money Mom said Grandpa and all those other old people paid to stay there, they could at least have installed an elevator.

The floors were like the ones at school too, easy to clean and the same putrid greenish-yellow; they gleamed under the fluorescent lights like some snotty ice-rink. Running shoes were required on floors like those. I once wore my favourite black shoes to school, the ones with the bows and spike heels, and made a complete fool of myself trying to get from class to class. Even our teachers wore runners (the better to escape with, my dear). But Grandpa's shiny, clean shoes were all leather, right down to their hard, smooth soles. At the time I wondered how he would ever survive there.

To add to the ambience, the air reeked of Pinesol laid on so thick that my eyes watered.

Mom, with Grandpa's clean laundry held to her chest schoolgirl-style, bulldozed her way up the stairs. Since Nana's death Grandpa hadn't let anyone else do his laundry for him, but he complained every time she didn't do it exactly as he liked it. She had that determined set to her shoulders that meant she was getting ready to roll into Grandpa's room and start interfering. He seemed to like it when she told him to put on his sweater, not to forget his scarf, and all the other bits of advice she dished out. It drives me nuts when she does that.

At the top of the stairs a long hall stretched out, broken by evenly spaced dark brown doors. The walls were a faded green that was probably once called leaf. Each door had a number, black on gold and cut on an angle, the cheap kind that you peel paper from the back and stick to whatever you need to label. Door number fourteen was open a crack. Mom knocked loudly. You never knew when Grandpa would decide to turn his hearing aid off. What you could be sure of is that halfway through a conversation with him he'd ask you to stop while he turned his ears on. Then he'd ask you to start over again from the beginning.

"Is that you, Marg?" Grandpa wheezed. Mom bullied her way in and I squeezed in behind her. Grandpa was sitting on a skinny bed with a brown metal headboard. The bed took up at least half the space in the ridiculously small room. The walls were the same faded green as the hallway. Grandpa's hands gripped his knees. It looked like he had to keep his arms straight, like the safety brace on the lid of my old toy box, so he wouldn't collapse.

"How are you feeling today, Dad?" Mom asked.

"Not bad, considering."

"Here's your laundry." Mom turned and, without taking a step, laid it on the top of the dresser. The veneer along the bottom was chipped and peeled, and the top was decorated with scratches and water stains. How many times had it seen the few worn belongings of some old person carefully folded away only to be later removed and replaced by someone else's things?

Mom turned again and bent to kiss Grandpa's grey, stubbly cheek. Now for some grandfathers a grey, stubbly cheek might have been normal but not for mine. I hadn't even known he was sick the whole time I was at music camp. Now I could see it had been worse than anyone told me. As usual, Mom and Dad hadn't wanted to spoil my good time with bad news. But how did they think I felt when I came home? Lousy, that's how. What if he had died?

I took three steps and bent to kiss his cheek, scratching my lips on his whiskers. He smelled different, stale, like an old washcloth with a touch of mildew. I turned and sat on the end of the bed. The blue-grey wool blanket was pulled tightly over sheets so smooth they looked like they'd been glued there. He'd made his bed like that since army camp in the First World War. Some habits never die. Their very existence serves as a rite to ensure the safe passage of another day.

"Oh, Sue, I'm so glad you came!" Grandpa said. My eyes mirrored his, blue as the mountains of the Scottish highlands where he had been born.

"This is a sad state of affairs I've gotten myself into," he sighed. "But I'll soon be out of here." He pushed his shoulders back and took a deep breath that ended in a repressed cough. I glanced at Mom. Her face was turned and she was staring out the window. Her pink lipstick looked like it would flake off her tight lips. Her arms in her favourite beige wool sweater set were wrapped across her chest straitjacket-style.

"I'm afraid I can't even offer you a cup of tea." Grandpa gripped his legs. His grey flannel pants didn't hide how thin he was. Just old skin loosely clinging to old bone.

A picture of Grandpa as a young man sits on Mom's dresser at home. Once he told me with pride that, when he was young, guys who were into dressing well were called dandies. He looks straight out at you from the photo with eyes that seemed to say, "I'm someone you should be watching 'cause I'm going places." His hair was orange, the colour of a maple leaf in September — though I'd never seen it any colour other than white. His smile was self-confident and easy. His foot rested on the running board of a shiny dark car. The suit he wore seemed to be light grey. Since it's a black and white photo I like to think it was really a soft yellow, like the primroses that grew in the shade of his garden. Nobody in our town had a garden as beautiful as my Grandpa's. In the photo his right hand rested on the top of a thin cane, the kind that was fashionable for "stepping out." A handsome guy, I'd say. Pretty full of himself, too.

"It's a lovely day, Dad. Would you like to go for a drive?" Mom turned from the window, smiling thinly. Through the unwashed glass and screen I could see the dirty, yellow siding and black roof of the house beside this building. What an ugly view. Imagine spending your last years staring out at that.

"Just give me a chance to get cleaned up, Marg, and we'll be off. It'll feel good to get out and get some air."

"I'll go tell the nurse," said Mom. She manoeuvred carefully past our legs and out of the room.

Grandpa got up and shuffled to the washbasin in the corner near the door. He lowered himself into the old, varnishless wooden chair in front of the sink as if it would cut into his flesh if he moved too fast. A year ago he could walk all the way downtown from his apartment on Victoria Street to have a cup of tea and a chat with his cronies, as he called them, at Turk's Restaurant.

He peered steadily into the mirror propped against the taps, frowned, and rubbed his hand slowly over the offending whiskers.

"Oh, I'm quite a mess, that's for sure," he sighed. "That bout in the hospital was almost the death of me. And if that didn't just about kill me the food they served nearly did. They couldn't even make a decent cup of tea!" He reached out and took his comb from the top of the chipped enamel sink. The veins that crossed over the bones of his hand moved like purple-blue worms writhing under his skin. He pulled the comb through his hair, smoothing it back from his forehead. A scab glared hotly above his left eyebrow near his hairline. Some kind of skin cancer. The doctor removed it every few months but it just grew back. It never seemed to get any bigger so I assumed it wasn't deadly.

Once combed, his hair swooped back like a snowdrift, soft and full and elegant. I hope my hair looks like that when I am eighty-four. That will be in sixty-nine years. Then I'll have sixteen years left. Grandma, my Dad's mom, and I made a vow to make it to one hundred. Nana died a long time ago of a brain tumor. I prayed and prayed and prayed for her to get better. Didn't the Bible say: "Ask and you shall receive?" Well, I asked and she died anyway. Maybe I hadn't used the right formula. Maybe God had failed me, instead of me failing Him. Probably He had other plans and my prayers didn't figure in them. Maybe our prayers are a nuisance God just has to put up with, like the kid in the supermarket begging her mom for candy at the check-out counter.

Don't get the idea I'm a fanatic or anything. I was raised to be a good Presbyterian, that's all. Grandpa is so proud of being Presbyterian. He seems to think he'll sit closer to God because of it. When he was younger and his voice was strong he sang in the choir. Mom says he had a beautiful baritone voice. Mom used to sing alto in the choir when she was younger. I remember sitting between Nana and Grandpa trying my best to keep still when what I really wanted to do was race down the gently sloping red carpet that led to the communion table. I thought my mom, way up in the choir loft, was as beautiful as an angel. Now I sing in the choir. Soprano. I have a good voice but I'm not beautiful like Mom. My nose is too long and I don't have very nice skin. Mom's always telling me to hold my head up, but I don't like to have all those people looking at me.

"It'll feel good to clean all this off." Grandpa rubbed his whiskers again as if hoping, by some strange magic, they'd disappear on their own.

Beside the basin there was a glass shelf where he'd put his shaving kit. The shelf had sharp pointy edges. You've got to wonder at the intelligence of putting something like that in the room of an old person. The chances of someone that age slipping and falling and possibly slicing part of their face off on it are about on a par with the chances of my face breaking out right before giving a class presentation.

Underneath the shelf a familiar towel and facecloth were draped neatly over a rusty metal towel holder. Grandpa reached for his old razor, nearly upsetting his balance as he took it from the shelf. He inserted the little beige plug into the sink and turned on the hot water. Steam filled the air and fogged the mirror, making Grandpa look like he was under water, drowning.

He took the soap from the pink plastic soap dish at his left. He rubbed his hands together and made a thick lather that he smeared over the lower half of his face and neck. With the razor in his right hand he squinted hard and leaned toward the mirror. His hand shook and I found I was holding my breath. Slowly I released it and concentrated on breathing normally. He pulled the skin on his right cheek taut with his left hand and tried to scrape off the whiskers. After the second unsuccessful try a long breath escaped with a whistle through his nose. He had been holding his breath too. Slowly he lowered his arm and rested it heavily on the edge of the sink. His eyes were shiny and wet. Suddenly I didn't know where to look. Oh, please Grandpa, I silently begged, don't cry.

"Sue, do you think you could do this for me? I just can't seem to get it going." His voice was shaky.

"Of course I can, Grandpa!" I jumped from my spot on the end of the bed. "I'll have it done in no time." I tried to sound cheerful, but this was not a good time. Not that I minded doing it. No, not at all. It's just that it was terrible to see Grandpa like that.

"Nice and smooth, eh, Sue?" Grandpa said and winked up at me with reddened lids.

I had never been this intimate with Grandpa before. It was a real privilege that he asked me to do this. He could have asked Mom. I had also never shaved a man's face before. I have shaved my legs and armpits since I was twelve. I remember the first time I shaved my legs. I was camping with Mom, Dad, and my younger sister, Kath. I borrowed Mom's razor and, with only the towering fir trees watching, performed the operation outside the tent door. The water in the turquoise dish tub came from the pump at the edge of our campsite. It was freezing cold, a murky yellow, and smelled like blood even before I started. My technique hasn't improved much since then. I always end up with a nick or two at my ankles or behind my knees.

Please God, I pleaded (candy time at the check-out counter again) don't let me nick Grandpa. Things were bad enough as it was.

After reapplying the foam to his face and neck I pulled the skin on his left cheek tight with the flattened fingers of my left hand. For once I was grateful for my chewed nails. At least I didn't have to worry about poking him. Gently I scraped the razor across the stubble. A rosy path appeared flanked by bluish white. Over and over I scraped the razor across his thin, loose flesh, retrieving it from unshaven slovenliness. His upper lip emerged, pink and twitching as if testing the air. And then the neck.

"Tilt your head back Grandpa, please."

"Careful there now, Sue," he said. Our eyes met and he smiled. "A nick there would certainly spoil the job."

The veins in his neck pulsed unbearably close to the blade. His Adam's apple, like a stone stuck in his throat, threatened to jump up and knock the razor flying. Slowly and carefully I scraped away at his neck, obliterating the last stubbly grey whiskers.

The sink was rimmed with white gunky soap. There was hair swimming around in it and it looked gross. I pulled the chain attached to the plug, and the water slowly disappeared down the drain with a hungry slurp, leaving behind a rind of whiskers. Using a white washcloth decorated with someone else's monogram and some hot water, I wiped the basin clean. I refilled the sink and took Grandpa's clean, brown facecloth from the towel rack. With the hot cloth I washed the last bits of soap from Grandpa's face then stepped back and eyed the job. Pretty good and no nicks. Thanks, God. Grandpa looked critically in the mirror turning his head to the left, the right, then up to peer under the chin.

"Hand me my after-shave lotion, Sue."

I handed him a bottle of liquid, blue as poison, from the shelf. He splashed it onto his left hand and then rubbed it over his jaw and neck. A sharp, clean smell chased all the other smells from the room.

"That's lovely," sighed Grandpa. "I feel so much better. Thank you, dear." He took my hand and patted it softly. His fingers were cool and smooth like silk.

"It was my pleasure, Grandpa." I was sorry to see the moment coming to an end.

"Hand me my sweater and cane, would you, Sue?"

Mom walked in just as Grandpa stood up. He rested his weight on his sturdy cane and stood as straight as his back would hold him. His head was held high.

"Dad, you look wonderful!"

"Thank you, Marg. Shall we go now?" He reached back and squeezed my hand.

He crossed the hall shuffling his feet. At the top of the stairs he put his left hand firmly on the green metal banister, and with his right he gave me his cane. Then he put his hand on Mom's arm and together they descended the stairs.

"Careful there, Dad . . . " Mom muttered. "Watch your step . . . not too fast now . . . "

Behind them I swung the cane, bumped the rubber end and counted each step. It took forever and forty-two steps to get to the bottom. Finally I returned the cane to Grandpa and hurried to open the door. It was heavy and swung outward slowly. Sunlight poured over us, a golden baptism. Grandpa looked up and smiled, turning his face in the warmth.

"I'll get the car," Mom said. She put Grandpa's hand on my arm. His breath was coming in great heaves that he eased through pursed lips. By the time Mom returned with the car, it had become a mild puffing and blowing. I opened the car door and held it for him as he struggled into the front seat and settled his cane between his bony knees. Then I swung into my usual spot behind the passenger and buckled myself in.

"Dad, do up your seatbelt," Mom ordered. I've often wondered if she will never get over the fact that, despite the statistics, there are still people who don't want to wear seatbelts.

"Blasted thing constricts my breathing," Grandpa complained.

"I'm not moving until your seatbelt is buckled," said Mom. "Here, let me help you."

Grandpa made a harrumphing noise then obediently leaned back and allowed Mom to adjust the strap and buckle him in.

"Where would you like to go?" Mom asked as she turned the key in the ignition. A well-oiled purr wrapped itself around us.

"Oh, anywhere," said Grandpa. Then, "How's about out Garden Hill way?"

"Sounds good to me," Mom said. "We'll stop somewhere for a cup of tea later." The car pulled away from the ugly red-brick building and, after shimmying through a few back streets, turned onto the deep green cool of Ontario Street. We continued past the gas stations and flourishing fast-food businesses that attached themselves like ticks to the outer layer of town, and headed towards Highway 28. As we started to cross the bridge that passed over Highway 401, Mom said, "The nurse told me they won't be able to keep you there, Dad. That home is meant for people who can still take care of themselves. She said you need to be someplace where they can give you more attention."

"Let's talk about it later, Marg," said Grandpa staring straight ahead. A deep sigh filled the car and the silence that followed pulsed loudly in my ears. Did this have to happen? I really never thought old age would touch him. Not this way. My eyes stung and my throat was so tight I felt like I was choking. Finally a noise from the front passenger seat shattered the silence. An old Scottish hymn, barely heard at first but gathering strength with each breath, came from deep inside Grandpa supported by something stronger than his failing body. The hair on my bare arms stood on end. Grandpa is the only person I know who can whistle and warble at the same time. Mom's shoulders stiffened. Even at that moment she hated it when Grandpa did that. But I loved it, especially at that moment. Brushing tears from my eyes I remembered the feel of rasping whiskers, loose, soft flesh, and an intimacy as delicate as a hummingbird I once held in the palm of my hand.

The Identity

Terry Thulien

Based on a true story from the Journals of
Alexander Henry the Younger

Put him in here boys. Watch his head!" Master Henry's voice is seasoned with alarm.

"Be ye sure, sir?"

"What do ye mean, lad? Why would I not put him in my room?"

"Could be he has the pox!"

"I've seen smallpox before." Henry shakes his head. "He's not got the dread disease."

"But can ye be sure, sir?" Fear emphasizes my friend's Gaelic accent.

"Feel his head, lad. He is not so hot as to give evidence of smallpox. And his skin is very clear for a young boy. If it were the pox he would be covered in pimples, then scabs, and before long his skin would fall off."

"Put him on de bed, sir?" The big black man called Pierre looks at me with measured empathy.

"Right, Pierre. He's a small one. Shouldn't fill no more than half the bed."

"But he is heavy."

I know the pain is about to begin again. I pull my knees into my stomach, hoping the anguish will be bearable this time.

"Stop your moaning now, son. We've moved you into my room." Through my pain I hear the soothing voice of the post-master. For a moment I let myself believe that everything will be all right. He tucks a goose-down pillow beneath my head and wipes the sweat from my brow.

"If it is not the pox, what do you think sickens de boy?"

"I know no more than you, Pierre. Did you see him cross the river from the Hudson's Bay fort?"

"Yes. I was out by de river talking with Red Cloud. He say his family is hungry. I ask him why he run out of pemmican so early in winter. Like I did not already know."

"We'll take care of Red Cloud later, Pierre." Henry turns to Angus. "What about you, lad? Were you the one who brought him over?"

"Aye, sir." He lowers his head. "My name be Angus."

"One of Hugh Heney's Orkney lads?"

"Aye, sir. Both me and John."

"So tell me what you know. How did this illness start?"

"We were in the storage room, sir," Angus looks at the snow on his boots. I know he feels uncomfortable discussing Hudson's Bay business with the master of the North West Company post. "John was helpin' me find a sour pelt that was causin' some discomfort to the other traders." He looks at me.

"Go on, Angus?" Henry pushes.

"We were workin' and all of a sudden he started a-moanin'. He curled up for about a minute, then he straightened and appeared to be better. I didn't question him. I thought maybe his stomach was a-turnin'. You know, sir, it's mighty hard for a good Scot to go without a bowl of thick oatmeal for so many months. Pemmican tends to stop things up a wee bit."

"I know what you mean, Angus. Tell me more about John. But wait! The pain has seized the lad again."

They watch me twist.

"I will not question him for the time being. Perhaps we can sort through this strange illness without putting more stress on the boy."

I close my eyes. The pain has subsided, but I know it will return. I am an ignorant Orkney but I know the course set before me.

The men pull stools from the outer room and gather round my bed as if they have all day to identify my ailment. Henry nods to Angus.

"The two of us go right back to work." Angus speaks more softly now, as if reluctant to continue. "I find the offensive pelt and I'm about to toss it out into the snow when John starts a-moanin' again. The affliction lasted for about a minute, but this time I see terror in his eyes."

"Terror, you say?"

"Aye, sir. It was like he realized at that moment what be wrong with him."

I hold my breath. I know the men are looking down at me.

"What happened after that, Angus?" There's a slight change in the tone of Henry's voice.

"I say to him, 'What be wrong with ye, John?' And he says to me, 'Nothing but a wee bellyache.' I suggested he get some essence of peppermint from Mr. Heney, but he shakes his head. Then he tells me he wants to come across the river to the North West fort."

"So you brought him across and left him on my doorstep."

"Aye, sir, while I waited around the corner. I came a-runnin' when I heard you call for your man, Pierre."

I stir, for I know the pain is about to begin again.

"Calm yourself now, lad," Mr. Henry speaks gently, though I do not respond to his kindness.

"You men can go now. I'll watch over the boy. But go fetch Tall Woman before you return to your work. She may know of a herb that will help the lad's pain."

I am left alone with post-master Alexander Henry. I think about nothing until the pain subsides.

Henry's hands are warm. They slip across my neck as he unties my scarf. He pulls away the wool of my Hudson's Bay coat and begins to unfasten the button on the collar of my shirt. Without thinking my hands fly to my neck. I clutch my clothing with tight fists.

"What is it, boy? I only mean to loosen your clothing so you'll be more comfortable."

I don't answer him. He shakes his head and leaves my heavy clothing wrapped about my body. To my relief he turns his attention to the small warming stove in the corner of the room.

An overwhelming fear fills my heart as I watch the man stuff the stove with buffalo chips. Alexander Henry is a man given to kindness. That is why I came to him. But I know without a doubt that if a situation warrants severe punishment he is more than able to enforce it.

What chastisement will he inflict upon me when he determines the root of my ailment? I cover my face with my hands. My fingers fall across my eyes like prison bars. Will it be my fate to spend the remainder of my days locked away in the *pot au buerre*? Or will I suffer a far worse fate than imprisonment? I shake my head to dislodge the nightmare. Surely the post-master would not send me to the *cantine salope*!

Angus bursts into the room as once again my body is seared with pain. "Tall Woman is not in the fort, sir." He looks at me, swallows, then continues his report. "She be downstream. Her man shot a deer and she is dressing the animal." He looks at me again.

I see frustration in his eyes. Angus has become a close friend over the past six months. Will the pain he feels, when he discovers that I have used him in my deception, be anything like the pain I feel at this moment?

"Go find her!" Henry orders. "The lad's discomfort is growing more intense."

The agony slips away as drops of sweat curl around the curves of my cheeks.

Angus and I left the Bay together six months ago, aboard a long birchbark canoe. Down the Albany River and into Lake Superior we sat side by side, as eight voyageurs paddled us through every sort of hell imaginable to man. At least I thought thus until this hour, for an ordeal worse than hell has now descended upon me.

We walked the trail together, my friend and I, to Grand Portage. Then again we travelled by canoe across tree-framed lakes and down dazzling streams to the shallow inland sea called Lake Winnipeg.

Angus and I were ordered to head south from the lake, down the Red River to Pembina. My heart sank when I learned of my posting. I wished to go further south, to Grande Fourches.

I know the pain is descending upon me again. I endure, as I know I must.

I wipe away the tears that are mingling with the sweat from my brow. I know it is not the manner of a man to cry, for I have watched the actions of men closely and have learned to copy them.

"Go ahead and weep, my boy." Henry speaks in soothing terms as he touches my cheek. I try not to pull sharply from his gentleness.

"I have a small bottle of pembina juice left from the berries of summer. I will get you a few sips. Perhaps it will ease your belly somewhat."

I nod my gratefulness, knowing the cranberry juice will help.

In the desolation of the small, unadorned room I force my mind from the direction in which it desires to travel. I must not give in to my emotions.

I close my eyes and pretend to feel the soft breezes of the Orkney Islands blowing across my face. If only I had remained in the land of my birth! There is no place in the world like the islands north of Scotland. No place. The mild ocean currents warm the region, causing the land to be gentle on its people. The long, sun-filled nights of summer and the darkness that covers the land in winter — I yearn for the seasons of my homeland.

My imagination fails me as I look about my surroundings. To call the building in which I am presently imprisoned a "big house" is a joke of the cruelest kind. It is but a log shack cut from the earth and left to stand unprotected in the ferocious winter wind of Rupert's Land.

Henry returns, carrying a mug, but he stops at the foot of the bed as once again I am engulfed with pain.

The pain does not completely leave me this time. It lingers in the small of my back. With enormous effort I curl forward to drink from Henry's mug.

"Try to relax, son. Tall Woman will be here soon. She is wiser in the treatment of pain than I." Mr. Henry turns and walks to the window. He remains thus positioned, though certainly not for the sake of vision. He is uncomfortable, as am I.

Unlike Mr. Henry, I fear the arrival of Tall Woman. She will not be fooled. I know her well. The Indian woman is the country wife of a Scottish trader. Until last summer she and her man lived in the far north, at Fort Chipewyan. She bore him four children in the land of her ancestors.

My thoughts are interrupted by pain. Henry glances at me, then turns away. I must continue my diversion.

That Tall Woman is now in the land of the Saulteaux Indian is an oddity. A country wife is usually left behind when a trader moves on to another post or returns to his homeland.

I do not understand this, how a man can love a woman for years, then trade her off to someone else or simply desert her.

I have held Tall Woman in great respect since I learned of her background. Not only is she greatly loved by her husband but she is also a very courageous woman to leave behind her own people and venture into a new region.

I told her one day of my admiration toward her. Tall Woman's reply to my praise was almost a rebuke. She told me my respect should not be based on her exploits or her ability to acquire a man, but rather on the good qualities she demonstrates.

The pain is even greater this time. I did not think it possible.

As it releases me, I am seized by panic. Tall Woman will arrive at my bedside very soon. Or perhaps she has guessed my secret and knows my travail will continue for some time longer.

I have talked with the wise woman more than safety allowed. There are no white women in the west and most of the other wives do not speak English. Tall Woman distracted me with stories of meeting Peter Pond and Alexander Mackenzie. She was at Fort Chipewyan seventeen years ago, in the summer of 1789, when twenty-five year old Alexander Mackenzie went in search of the famed North West Passage.

Tall Woman recalled accompanying her brother on long journeys south, into the land of the treacherous Blackfoot Indian, to obtain bags of pemmican.

A wave of agony again washes over me. I can feel myself growing numb to the pain, for it is no longer diminishing to a comfortable extent.

I try to recall more of Tall Woman's stories, but my mind is pulled into forbidden territory. In my weakened condition, I can not hold it back from where it craves to travel.

I can wrestle no longer.

With a great sob, I surrender my false identity!

I shed my male disguise.

Suddenly the agony in my heart is more severe than the pain engulfing my body.

Fear had kept me from examining the source of this torment, but I have passed beyond fear. I am now in a world outside myself.

I thought I suffered because of my great love for John Scarth. He refused to offer me his family name so I took his Christian name. How deceived I have been! It is rejection that has birthed this great pain.

Words of love were exchanged between John and myself. I was sure his words were true. All these months I have refused to admit that John discarded me, for I feared that I would grow to hate him for what he has done.

He sought the warmth and comfort of my body, telling me I must return his love by trusting him. He took freely of my soul.

Anger swells within me and mingles with the severe anguish of another heavy contraction.

My mind clears and I see something I have not seen before. I did not love John as I had professed. My motives were as selfish as his. Love was not the reason I allowed him to invade my body.

I was not searching for love. What I sought was an identity.

I am but an ignorant Orkney girl. I was nothing until John poured his attentions upon me. He made me worthy.

"The lad is in here, Tall Woman." Mr. Henry's words startle me. I had forgotten his presence.

The Indian woman moves to my side and begins to pull away my sweat-laden clothes.

"He grew distressed when I attempted to disrobe him," Henry explains.

I do not fight Tall Woman's firm touch. My time has come. I feel a burst of moisture surround my lower body.

"What be wrong with the poor lad?" Angus lingers in the doorway of the room.

Tall Woman looks down at me. Her eyes are full of gentleness and understanding. She knows my secret agony.

Drawing strength from the Indian woman I turn to postmaster Henry.

"Please do not deal harshly with me, sir." I speak clearly.

"Why would I show anything but kindness to you, lad?"

"I have deceived you, sir. I am not John Fubbister but Isabel Gunn, a wretched Orkney girl who is about to give birth."

Henry's face is as blank as a cloudless sky. I cannot read his reaction to my startling confession. He backs away from my bed.

My vision falls upon Angus. I search his face for anger, but find none. His face is awash with concern.

"See her through, Tall Woman." Henry grasps Angus by the arm and leads him from the room.

"I have waited, my child," Tall Woman quickly removes my clothing and covers me with a fresh smelling cloth. "Time has left you unprepared."

"You knew all along, didn't you, Tall Woman?"

"Yes."

She rubs my abdomen as I writhe with pain.

"What is this deception you have forged, child?"

"It was an elaborate plan. But conceived in the mind of a fool."

She shakes her head. "Do not be harsh with yourself."

I groan gently as she works her strong fingers into my stomach. "His name was John Scarth. He took what he wanted, knowing he would soon be leaving Scotland. When I learned that he had no intention of taking me with him to Rupert's Land, I pieced together a scheme so that I might follow him."

Tall Woman gently determines the progress of my labour while another contraction grips my body.

Slowly I pull myself from the black abyss of pain and continue my story. "I knew the Hudson's Bay Company would not hire a young girl so I decided to assume a false identity. I cut my hair and dressed myself in the clothing of a boy. When I presented myself to the Company they were more than willing to accept my indentureship. So as a servant of the Hudson's Bay I boarded the *Prince of Wales* and sailed for Rupert's Land. John continued to enjoy my company until he learned that it was his child within my womb that was the cause of my lingering illness. He made a hasty departure to his posting at Grand Fourches."

The words rip from my throat as the most vicious pain thus far assaults my frail body. Tall Woman massages my belly until I again breathe normally. She turns and removes a small pouch of liquid from her bag.

I accept the moisture. In my numb state I do not taste it.

"A mash from the painted trillium plant," she explains. "It is strong, but it will speed your delivery."

Before I can continue my story, anther contraction blinds me.

"It will not be long now, my child. Does John know you are in Pembina?"

"Yes, he knows." Tears fill my eyes. "I thought he would arrive before my time." I cannot control the sobs that shake me.

Again I am assaulted by pain, but this time it is unlike anything I have suffered so far. I feel myself pushing, though not willfully.

"Have you thought about this baby?" Tall Woman touches my wet cheek as I regain a measure of composure.

"No," I reply without thought. Since the day I learned of my pregnancy, I have refused to think of the weight within my womb.

Though I have been achingly aware of its presence every minute of every day.

Only once did I consider . . . But I cannot think of such things now.

The agony returns and I push until I feel as if I will explode.

"I can see the head." Tall Woman's voice is calm.

Suddenly my mind clears, and for a few seconds the pain detaches itself from my body.

My child is about to enter this world. A child who is more important than anything else in my life.

A strength surges through me as I prepare to push again.

"Press down!" Tall Woman coaxes. "Keep pushing!"

A most extraordinary sensation grips my body as the child gushes from my womb. It's unbelievably painful but incredibly thrilling.

The world is silent as I listen. Never in my entire life have I craved so intensely for a sound. A cry.

I attempt to lift myself, but my body has not completed its cleansing.

I hear Tall Woman. She is whispering soft words. A prayer, I think.

My heart nearly leaps from my shattered body as a spectacular sound fills the room. The voice of my child peals forth like the ringing of a mighty bell of joy.

Tall Woman places the squalling infant upon my flattened stomach. "He is a perfect child."

I reach for him and stroke his blood-caked hair. There are no words to describe how I feel toward this tiny human. I have never felt such love. I cannot bear to think that I had once mixed the dangerous herbs that would have caused this wonder to die within my womb.

"A creation of God." Tall Woman gently wipes a lock of moist hair from my forehead.

I am taken by surprise as the definition of love suddenly becomes strikingly clear to me.

What I feel for my child is completely unselfish.

In my relationship with John, we were both pursuing our own desires. John sought physical comfort and I sought a person who would give me a sense of self-worth. But love is not self-seeking.

An unwanted sadness circles my heart as I consider the consequence of this unselfish love toward my baby. What kind of life can I, a homeless, destitute girl, give this tiny boy?

I do not want to use this child to give myself yet another identity.

A tear dribbles down my cheek as I turn to Tall Woman. "Do your people have a way in which a family can care for the child of another woman?"

"We have a ceremony of adoption." Her eyes search my very heart. "The Indian people always want the best for their children."

I am not ready to decide if my love is strong enough for such a sacrifice. This love is so new to me, and my future so uncertain.

I push these thoughts aside as Tall Woman pillows my back with blankets, then hands me my child wrapped in soft doe-skin. Cradling him to my overflowing heart, I watch him obtain nourishment from my body.

A warm tear of love drops from my cheek and falls upon his tiny fist. No greater wonder will I ever witness.

Claire

Karin Galldin

Some people float by in a hazy cloud and only when it is too late do they turn around. Life for them is a series of dreams linked by daytime occurrences. But me, I always kept my head up. I was never satisfied with a trace of perfume, or footprints marked in snow. No, I wanted to see their faces.

Men I constantly pursued; perhaps I was searching for an angel. Not so much now but in my earlier years I would be attracted by a sensual curve of the mouth. It alone would tempt me and haunt me in my mirror. I would adopt personae to please these unknown men, as a woman wears different pastels to appease the gods of spring. It is ironic that, among all these empty icons, Claire's smile is the one I still remember . . .

Before those turbulent seasons of struggle in which the child becomes a woman, my loves were simple. I was a gap-toothed, merry urchin, always teasing, always laughing. Rarely did I cultivate obsessions; I can recall only one now in my old age. I was six, and the object of my affections was so enticing that he prompted me to pack a backpack and to attempt the long trudge to his house. Unfortunately, my mother found me trekking across the park, and I was forbidden to see my lovely sweetheart. I have been more successful with my endeavours since then.

When I was in the midst of high school Claire moved into my neighbourhood of veteran trees and venerable senior citizens. I was walking the dog around the block when she emerged from her house, dark and solemn. Not knowing what to say, I just stood in the street and looked. She was gathering books up from under a birch tree and, as she stooped, her black hair swept across her cheek like water. Self-consciously, I ran my hand over my unruly curls. Then she straightened up and turned towards me. I stared in astonishment at her appearance. She was wearing a long, black skirt with ragged edges, a shining turquoise blouse, and dozens of beaded necklaces. Small, silver men hung from her ears. As she waited there under the tree a velvety cat wove between her ankles; she scooped it up and held it close.

"There, there, Greymalkin," I heard her say in a soothing tone. She was gazing at me expectantly, as if I was about to burst out in song, as though I was on a stage. I became increasingly uncomfortable and so moved on, and when I got home I told my mother about the gypsy who was living down the street.

Claire was in my English class at school. I grew to recognize her as an unpredictable, intriguing girl, but we were not friends. I was caught up in my flighty existence of dark basements and scratching records and boys who were eager to the point of annoyance. I wasn't lacking in attention, whereas Claire . . . I don't know what she did. Sometimes at night I would walk by her house, dizzy with my youth, and her profile was visible through the curtains. My mother dismissed her as a flake, but when I was placed with her for a poetry assignment, I learned to see her as more.

I had been declared a disaster by my teacher, for my poetry was erratic, harsh, and disjointed. At first I did not see any wisdom in my being paired with Claire. She came to the desk beside mine and announced that she was not partial to reading her work aloud. I, having a notebook full of blank pages, reiterated that I had nothing to share. She pursed her lips and stared at me so intently that I avoided her gaze. Then Claire sighed and began to speak. Oh, of all the music that I have heard in my life, nothing was as lovely as the words spilling out of her mouth. I sat transfixed, watching her bottom lip twist and turn, and I aged more that half hour than I had all year.

From then on, Claire embodied magic. I spent countless afternoons curled up on her bed as she romanced me with her poetry. We would lie, tangled together, on the grass in her backyard in the evening, and we would read each other's futures in the stars.

One afternoon while she and I were eating popsicles, she said pensively, "You know, Anne, I'm not sure I like boys." And I giggled because I didn't know how to respond to that. She glanced at me — her eyes were so round — and continued: "I mean, if society hadn't always forced the idea that girls like boys and vice versa, don't you think people would be falling in love with whoever, no matter what gender?"

I went silent, not understanding her words, nor seeing their relevance. Claire had a strained look on her face. Then the strangeness was broken by her gasp.

"Oh!" she exclaimed, "I've dripped on myself!" As she rushed inside to wash the red blotches out of her shirt, I stood up to leave. That day left a bitter taste in my mouth.

Today, as I look through my old poetry, I realize that most of it was written for Claire. She sat by my side and encouraged me with a touch or a smile as I faltered. Together we became the *writers* of the class; I entertained them with witty, sarcastic pieces while she seduced them with slyly crafted odes. But it couldn't stay like that, could it? I guess Claire's world was made of finer stuff.

Perhaps I never knew that girl with the moon in her eyes. Maybe her poetry was a false front. I just know that what she said one night almost broke my heart, and my response, I'm sure, shattered hers.

Our houses were near a river. Claire and I had never yet walked down there, and so one balmy summer night we left her house and headed in the direction of the water. The air was not particularly sticky, but as we strode through the trees a faint perspiration grew on my arms. I looked over at Claire, and she too had a wet sheen on her forehead. So we proposed to go for a swim. I haven't forgotten how the breeze wrapped itself around my unclothed body as we stood by the water's edge. As we waded into the cool river, I felt as though I was dissolving.

Claire moved her slim body through the current and together we swam farther out. Holding my hand as we treaded water, she began to speak, but I wasn't listening. The moon was casting golden images on the river's surface; I thought I was suspended in time. After immeasurable moments spent languishing in the depths, I stretched my body and floated towards shore. We crept out of the water and into the shadows.

"Are you ready?" Claire asked and I murmured, "Yes." She stepped out of the bushes.

We were standing face to face, when Claire stroked my face with her hand. I stepped back, startled.

"Don't . . . " she pleaded, "don't be afraid of me." I stood a step away from her, but it was as though I was seeing her from a great distance. "Anne . . . " she said.

I stared at her and I realized that I loved her, but I didn't know how to. My knees buckled under my weight.

"Anne," she whispered, "my poetry . . . it's about you . . . " And her face swam closer to mine. That moment, which I have replayed in my head millions of times, my courage left me. I turned away and began to take small, measured steps away from Claire, and in doing so, I failed her.

* * *

As I write this, I am an old woman. I don't know where
Claire is, but I think of her often. My husband, a man with
a curvaceous smile, doesn't realize that part of my love
belongs to a raven-haired stranger. I hope that she sees my
poetry, for, ironically, I am a poet. My first critically acclaimed
collection contained a small ode to a girl with curious, round
eyes — I think it is my best yet.

All my life, all my loves, it is she I search for on the streets,
among the faces of strangers. And when I see black hair
cascading like a waterfall, I take a second look.

The Bicycle

Jillian Horton

T ante Rose had promised me at a very early age that if I
studied my piano lessons very hard, she would some day
send me to New York to take lessons at a school where I would
study to become a concert pianist.

Tante Rose was a concert pianist. She was my mother's
older sister and my only aunt. She was tall, thin, and pale, with
thick, black hair that she wore cropped at the back of her neck.
Tante Rose was older than my mother but younger than my
father. She had never married, choosing instead to live a
private life with few acquaintances and still fewer friends. If I
ever asked her why she had chosen to remain single, she
laughed at me and said with a strange smile, "One day,
Hannah, you will understand why I made that choice. One day
you will understand how all choices are made."

When I was ten, Tante Rose had to give up performing as
a pianist. Arthritis, coupled with an old injury to nerves under
her collarbone, had sent her slender fingers curling in towards
themselves and had swollen her knuckles so they were like
knotted wood. She settled five blocks from us, in the North
End of Winnipeg. Every year she joined us for the Jewish
holidays of Passover, Yom Kippur and Chanukah. In her small
second-storey apartment, she gave piano lessons. She was my
teacher; I was her favourite pupil. Late some nights, Tante
Rose sat in our living room, drinking strong, black coffee and
talking with my parents. Though I was supposed to be at my
desk studying Hebrew lessons, I would press my face tight up

against the bedroom door and listen to hear Tante Rose tell my parents that I had a brilliant future as a concert pianist. I was eleven and in love with the life of music she described to me in so much detail. I dreamed of myself in flowing dresses with my long black hair grown out to my waist and a string of pearls at my throat. I saw myself travelling on airplanes to giant concert halls where people threw me flowers and chocolates and shouted my name. Tante Rose told my mother I had a special gift and that gift must be nourished. Tante Rose said if I made a few sacrifices and worked hard, I would be famous.

I practised every day for Tante Rose. After school I sat at the piano bench in the living room and studied finger exercises and simple Chopin études and little pieces by Bach and Mozart. Each was like a small, beautiful trinket to me. On Wednesdays I had my lesson with Tante Rose in her apartment. She had a grand piano that was like a magical animal; it was big and intriguing. She sat next to me on the bench, circling in the music when I played wrong notes, telling me when to play soft and when to play loud and sometimes speaking under her breath in Hebrew (which I knew) or Yiddish (which I did not). Always she looked pleased with my progress.

By my thirteenth birthday I was playing the music of Beethoven and Liszt with proficiency. I was a hard worker. I had to work if I was going to be a concert pianist like Tante Rose. I had no choice.

When I was fourteen I moved in to share Tante Rose's apartment. The move would allow me to devote all my free time to my studies in piano. It was decided that I would spend Saturday and Sunday night with my parents and brothers, but the rest of my week would belong to Tante Rose. I packed all my things into two big leather bags and carried them the five blocks to her apartment.

Tante Rose was at the apartment every day when I arrived from school. We sat down at four-thirty and worked together at the piano until seven at night. Then we stopped for soup and bread and tea. We began our work again at eight-thirty and went until ten. If I had homework it had to be done in the morning, before my classes began. Tante Rose demanded of me total commitment and devotion.

On Fridays, before sundown, Tante Rose insisted that I should close the piano and not open it again until nightfall on Saturday. She said that it was my duty to keep the Jewish Sabbath as a holy day for myself. On Friday nights she lit Sabbath candles, praying and singing the traditional songs while gently swaying back and forth to the music. She taught me to make the traditional Jewish bread, *challah*. Tante Rose braided the three strands of dough almost magically, her hands spinning the ropes around until she had two loaves that always seemed to come out of the oven crisp and perfect. The next morning, we got ready for synagogue, and we sat in the second row from the back. Tante Rose wore plain black dresses and crinkled soft scarves. She prayed in a soft voice and she knew all the prayers by heart. Saturday night, after the sun had gone down and we had eaten our evening meal, we went right back to work, feeling somehow refreshed for the week to come.

Once a month, Tante Rose took me to Eaton's downtown where she bought me clothes and shoes and things for school. My mother and father always seemed to be occupied with my three younger brothers. I once heard Tante Rose say to my parents, "Don't worry about Hannah. I will see that she gets all she needs in this life. I will take care of her."

At Eaton's, Tante Rose would buy me any dress I liked. She favoured long velvet skirts and white blouses with collars that made me feel like a queen. Once she bought me a gold chain with my name on it. "You are beautiful — my Hannah has grown up so fast," she said to me one day as we rode the bus home. "I will send you to New York in a year. You will be ready."

I worked hard that winter. It seemed as though I spent all my time practising. Sometimes it seemed there was nothing else in the world but Tante Rose and me and Tante Rose's piano. Tante Rose's piano became my friend, a familiar presence. When my fingers rushed over its flat white keys, from one end of the keyboard to the other, the instrument laughed like I was tickling it or cried like I was hurting it. Always Tante Rose was there with her pen, marking the wrong notes in red ink and promising me that soon I would be ready to study in America with the best teachers, to take my place in life. I listened to her trustingly, lovingly. I loved my Tante Rose so much.

Tante Rose had only ever forbidden me to do two things. One thing she forbade me to do was break the Sabbath in any way. This meant no piano, no homework, no playing with friends. The second thing she forbade me to do was ride on a bicycle. Tante Rose had hurt herself badly once when she was pitched from a bicycle. Her collarbone had been broken and it had never healed properly. She worried constantly about my having an accident that would cost me my career. It was perhaps an irrational fear on her part, but I knew it was important to Tante Rose. Consequently, she never allowed me even so much as to sit astride of my brother Avi's bicycle. I never thought much of this when I was young. It seemed a small price to pay for Tante Rose's devotion.

Yet in my mind there was always the memory of how it felt to ride a bicycle. Until my seventh birthday, I had navigated the neighbourhood streets on a two-wheeler, just like all of my friends. When I began to study piano with Tante Rose, she said

I must stop riding a bicycle. I stopped, but I still liked looking at bicycles, I liked touching them. My friends passed me on their way home from school, riding as fast as cars, then dragging their feet along the pavement to make themselves slow down, scuffing their good shoes. When the girls rode bicycles, their hair streamed out behind them and looked the way hair looks when you float motionless in the bath. I could never help staring at their hair. I had black hair like Tante Rose, only mine was long and braided from the temple down. I remembered what it felt like to have your hair fly out behind you. I wanted to feel the wind in my hair.

By my fifteenth birthday I was obsessed with the idea of riding a bicycle. I closed my eyes in class and thought about how it would be to be perched up on the leather seat and pedalling until I was out of breath. I looked at the pictures of the bikes in the Eaton's catalogue and I desperately, passionately, wanted a bicycle.

At the same time, I had begun to notice puzzling differences between myself and the other girls in my class. My friends Ilana and Leah, I observed, rode bikes and talked about movies and books and had dates and dance classes and Hebrew lessons. And after school, when Ilana and Leah went to Israel club or to the library, I went home to Tante Rose. Leah and Ilana sometimes telephoned me, but Tante Rose didn't like it when I talked on the phone because she thought it was a waste of time. Even on Friday, the one night when I did not practise, Tante Rose insisted that I stay *home* to celebrate the Sabbath. I felt lonely and isolated, increasingly aware of the differences between myself and girls like Ilana and Leah. I vowed that I would break my promise to Tante Rose. I would ride a bicycle, just once, to prove that I was at least a little bit like Ilana and Leah, to prove that I had some control over my own life. I needed somehow to prove this to myself.

I would have to decide on a time and a place. It was spring, and the melting snow meant I couldn't sneak a ride down the back lane because the lanes were too full of mud. I could ride through the park, but the park would be full of my friends, and someone might see me and tell Tante Rose. I would have to ride the bike on the path by the river, which was a ten-minute walk from my house. I would take my brother Avi's bike and if caught, I would say I had been returning it to him.

On a clear Friday afternoon in April, Tante Rose asked me to go to my parents' house to get my mother's recipe for potato kugel while she took a short nap. I walked there quickly, hurriedly. When I arrived and called out to my parents from the kitchen, Avi came around the corner of the stairs and told me they were at the dentist with my brother David. Then Avi went back up to his room.

Was this the chance I had been waiting for? I stood in the kitchen for a moment and thought very hard. Then I snuck out to the back yard, still in my velvet skirt and top, wearing my patent leather shoes with buckles. I felt my heart pounding inside my chest and I wondered about what would happen if Avi came out to get his bike and it was gone.

I pulled the bicycle, with its gleaming chrome handlebars and polished metal frame, out of the shed. My hands gripped it firmly; I saw my knuckles go white. It was such a strange thing to want to do, and yet, more than anything, I wanted to do it . . .

I pushed the bicycle to the end of my street and turned it around the corner. My family was occupied and Tante Rose was at home in bed, napping. I would be back at the house just before sundown, in time for Shabbat. Who would see me?

When I got to the corner I swung one of my legs over the bar at the top of the bike so that I was sitting on the seat. I put a hand on each of the brakes and flexed them. I had seen Avi use the brakes. I would use them too.

Placing a foot on each of the pedals, I strained with my knees to push each one down to the ground. I felt the wheels move as this happened, and a second later the bicycle was moving down the street, creeping slowly along the curb toward the road.

I wouldn't be able to feel the wind in my hair unless I was going faster, and so I pushed, harder and harder, against the pedals with my feet. I felt my legs sinking each time, then rising with the motion. I rode down to the river. I shook my head and felt my hair fly out behind me, and I went faster and faster until it was like a cape at my back. It was a good feeling. It was not as good as I thought it would be, but it was still a good feeling.

When I finally thought to look at my watch it said five-thirty. The sun would be going down in twenty minutes. With a sigh, I turned the bike back towards my house and rode it there slowly and reluctantly.

At the corner of Moon Street I noticed a man leaning up against a dark blue car. He had a beard and a round wide face. I had never seen him before. Out of my other eye I saw our neighbour, Mrs. Solomon, sitting on her front porch. She waved at me but I pretended not to see. As I passed the man with the beard, I had the strange feeling that he was pointing something at me. A minute later I turned around and saw that he had gone over to Mrs. Solomon and they were talking on her porch. I could barely make out their figures in the dim light.

It was late; the sky was visibly darkening. I locked the bike in the shed and went into the house to say hello to my parents. Tante Rose was in the kitchen with them; she looked irritated.

"Where do you go on Shabbos that you don't tell anyone where you're going?" she said in Hebrew.

"I had an errand to run," I replied hurriedly, coming over to kiss her and my mother on the cheek. I slid in next to Avi at the table.

"Go wash your hands and say the blessing," Tante Rose barked at me. "You should be home Friday right at sundown."

"I'm sorry," I said softly. Tante Rose cleared her throat. She got up to wash her hands for the meal and didn't mention my lateness again.

I looked at her during dinner and wondered if I should feel guilt for what I had done. I did not; I knew I would not do it again. I was only sorry that I had unconsciously marred the Sabbath. I thought to myself that in one evening I had broken both the promises I had ever made to Tante Rose.

The next morning Tante Rose and I dressed for synagogue as usual. We walked the two blocks in a friendly silence, the offenses of the previous night all but forgotten.

We entered the synagogue through the carved wooden doors at the front of the building. As we stepped inside, we each nodded hello to a number of our friends and acquaintances. I saw my schoolmates, Ilana and Leah, come toward us with broad smiles on their faces.

Ilana nodded to my aunt. "Hello, Miss Lutterman."

Leah turned to me. "Good Shabbos," she said, kissing me on the cheek. Then she giggled. "You're so famous now!"

I felt a wave of alarm rush through my body. I had not the slightest idea what Leah was talking about — until it suddenly occurred to me that Mrs. Solomon must have told everyone in the synagogue that she had seen me riding the bicycle. I smiled faintly at Leah and waved at her parents before taking my seat next to my aunt.

As soon as the service was over, I told Tante Rose I was not feeling well and would like to leave the synagogue quickly.

She looked at me with some sympathy. "We'll have our lunch and then you may have a short rest if you like." I nodded again. I felt sick to think that Mrs. Solomon might tell Tante Rose I had been riding the bicycle. I took a deep breath and let it out silently. I must have misunderstood Leah. It was all just a mistake.

When we arrived at Tante Rose's apartment, I unlocked the door with the key she had given me. As I pushed it open she bent down to pick up the Saturday newspaper from the floor. She seemed to stand stooped over, looking at it, for a long time.

"Hannah," she said in a barely audible voice. "Hannah, what is this?"

"That's the newspaper, Tante Rose," I said without thinking.

"Hannah, what is this photo on the front page of the newspaper?" I took the paper from her hand and froze suddenly.

In the upper left hand corner was a photo of me, Hannah Golandsky, riding a bicycle down Moon Street on Friday night at dusk. My hair was streaming out behind me and my velvet skirt was dangling around the pedals. In bold letters below was the caption *Spring is Finally Here . . .*

Tante Rose was absolutely silent. She pushed past me into the apartment without even looking at my face. I followed behind her, feeling numb. I shut the door.

"Tante Rose . . . " I started to say. She turned around and held up a finger for me to stop speaking. Then she stood with her hand across her mouth, forehead knotted.

She did not shout at me. Instead she came toward me so
that she was only a few inches from my face, and then she
spoke.

"I do not ask so much of you, Hannah. I buy the things you
need. I let you share my house. I have only two rules in this
house. You will be observant of the Sabbath and you will not
ride a bicycle." She held up the photo and waved it in front
of my face. "I do not make these rules up to test you. I ask you
to observe the Sabbath out of respect for your family and your
people. I ask you not to ride a bicycle because you have a gift.
I did not want you to foolishly jeopardize your gift." She threw
the paper down and turned away from me. "It is not the
danger of riding a bicycle that I am concerned about. It is the
discipline that you needed, Hannah, to stop yourself from
doing what you wanted to do. It is about discipline."

"But Tante Rose, why does it matter that I rode a bicycle?"
I said feebly, my voice trembling.

"It matters that you should take foolish risks." She stared
into my eyes and her face was red like fire. "When God gives
you a gift you cherish it. You showed me today that you do not
yet cherish yours."

"I just wanted to be like my friends," I said to her, my voice
nothing more than a whisper.

"And, Hannah, how many of your friends would like to be
like you . . . but will never be pianists because they lack a gift?"

I had no answer for Tante Rose. I stood staring at her,
feeling worse than I had ever felt in my life.

"Go home, Hannah," she said. "You cannot stay with me
any more."

My eyes opened in utter disbelief. Never had I dreamed
that Tante Rose would punish me in such a way.

"Tante Rose, I'm sorry! I had to know what it was like." I felt my insides begin to tremble and stared at the tips of my red shoes. "I wanted to be like the other kids."

"Then go!" she shouted at me. "Be like the other kids! You made your choice!"

I began to weep. "Don't make me go, Tante Rose."

We stood staring at each other for a long time; I remember thinking that there was not a trace of emotion on her face. Anger had hardened her skin into a mask of stone.

She went into her bedroom and locked the door behind her. Then a dreadful silence descended on the house. I stood still for a moment, then ran out the front door, down the stairs, and out of Tante Rose's building into the street. In my good shoes I ran the five blocks to my house and, breathless, entered the kitchen.

My father was standing over the sink drinking orange juice.

"Tante Rose said I can't live with her any more!" I sobbed out loud. "I rode the bicycle."

My father smiled slightly. "Yes, I know you rode the bicycle. We saw in the paper."

My brothers Avi and David came into the hall, laughing. "We saw your picture!" they shouted in unison.

I looked at my father. "Are you angry that I rode a bicycle on Shabbos?"

He looked thoughtful, then shook his head.

"Hannah, your mother is perhaps angry. But I would be lying if I said that I had never done something I should not have done on the Sabbath. I have no opinion."

I heard my mother's shoes scratching on the stairs and suddenly felt unable to face her or her anger. I backed out the door and ran blindly to the shed, grabbing Avi's bicycle. I threw myself onto the seat and rode down the back lane. I went down to the park and rode along all the streets and I even rode in front of Tante Rose's apartment but the blinds were closed.

I'm not strong like you, Tante Rose, I thought to myself. I can't give up everything because I have a gift.

When I came back to the house there was a white envelope on the table.

"What's that?" I asked my father.

He scratched his chin. "It's from your Aunt Rose."

I gasped. "She came here?"

"While you were riding the bike."

My face reddened. "What did she say?"

"Open the envelope," said my father.

My fingers shook as I pried the paper apart. I was shocked to find inside one airplane ticket to New York for the following week in April.

"Tante Rose said it was time for you to go, to audition at the school, and they will take you in September," said my father.

"Because she's angry at me?" I said, my eyes filling with tears.

"No," he said softly. "Not because she's angry. Just because it's time, Hannah."

"I'm not going," I said to him.

"Hannah," he said gently, "of course you'll go. You have a gift."

I shook my head; it was very clear to me now. "I am not going to New York."

My father sat at the table, looking at me. He seemed suddenly to sense that I had aged in the years I had been living with Tante Rose — that I had aged in a way he would never understand.

Tante Rose had said one day *I* would understand how choices were made. I understood as of that moment. I did not go to New York.

Tourists

Eileen Kernaghan

I guess you could say it all started when my computer-pal Freddy left one of his cryptic notes in my e-mail.

"So, Emily. Are you going to catch the Dark Goddess on holo tonight?"

"The *who?*" I zapped back.

"Selena, you lameoid. The Selena. Queen of Psyche-Music, Darling of the New Decadents, Goddess of the Post-Gothique."

Maybe I should explain that I'm not really up on the pop scene, being more into the classics — Lennon, Mozart, John Cage, people like that.

"Come on, Em, even *you* have to have heard of Selena. She's totally Extreme. A Selena concert is a Rare Event."

"So okay," I told him. "So maybe I'll watch."

Selena was more than Extreme. In terms of extremity, she was right off the Richter scale. Black velvet dress down to the floor and buttoned up to the chin but with a lot of the middle bits cut out. Jet-black hair, dead-white skin. The kind of enormous black eyes that romantic poets used to drown in. Hollow cheeks and jutting cheekbones like the models in the old fashion magazines my Aunt Veronica collects. Eyelids that drooped seductively, dark smudges underneath as though she hadn't slept for a week. Selena managed to look dissipated, and horribly unhealthy, and gorgeous, all at the same time.

And then there was the music. Selena's stage persona might be Nineteenth Century Decadent, but she was heavily into twenty-first century technology. Her compositions, as she explained, "were inspired by the psyche-sounds produced by the nervous systems of cold-blooded animals under stress." What came out of the synthesizer was the orchestrated anxiety of lizards in small cages, the shock and terror of bats bombarded by bright light, the primal need of a python ravenous for his next meal. It was brilliant, and horrible, and unlike any music I'd ever heard, or imagined.

Basically, I'm an acoustic kind of person, and my instrument is the flute. But like most musicians, I've played around with the new electronics that let you jack straight into the brain — your own or somebody else's — and translate all those random neural impulses into music, just as if you were using a keyboard. I'd nagged my mother into giving me a synthesizer for my thirteenth birthday, and after two years, if I do say so myself, I was getting pretty good. My suite for flute and psyche-sounds had won a big national prize for student compositions, and I'd done some neat little fugues, very multi-layered and complex, by sticking the electrodes on my mother's forehead when she was deep into one of her projects. (My mother is a biophysicist.)

Freddy was online before the studio audience had time to stop applauding. "So what did you think?"

"I think she's a vampire."

"That's what they say about all the Night People. It's just racism. Where's her fangs? "

"With what she gets paid, she can afford cosmetic surgery."

"Well, you can ask her yourself if she's a vampire. I have her e-mail address."

"Give me a break, Freddy."

"No lie. She answers her own mail. Some of it, anyhow. All the big celebs do that now — it keeps them in touch with their fans."

"So are you going to send her a message?"

"I already have. I told her about you, all the prizes you've won, how you're going to be the next big Psyche-Music star."

"Freddy, I'll kill you! How mortally humiliating! How can you be such a *jerk*?"

Even onscreen, Freddy managed to sound peevish. "Well, honestly, Emily, I won't try to do *you* any more favours."

"Please don't," I told him huffily.

"But I left her *your* e-mail address, just in case she wants to get in touch."

I didn't even look at my mail-box next day. I was busy finishing up a book I'd borrowed from my Aunt Veronica. She owns an antique store on Mall Level, and she's heavily into what she refers to as the Print Medium — not just ratty old magazines, but all kinds of old books, some of them going right back to the nineteenth century. This one was about the Victorian lady travellers who wandered all over the unexplored bits of the world — back in the days when there were unexplored bits, and you could still tramp around outside without air monitors and sunshields. I was especially taken with May French Sheldon, who travelled from Mombasa to Mount Kilimanjaro in 1891 to study the natives. She rode in a silk-lined palanquin, dined with tribal chieftains wearing a silk ball gown covered in rhinestones, and flew a flag that said Touch Me Not. Apparently nobody did.

I definitely feel I was born into the wrong century. It's like I'm serving a life sentence in a very comfortable high security prison. I can get on the Web and talk to anybody I like, anywhere in the world — yet at the same time I daren't put a foot outside my own apartment tower. (For example: Freddy lives three towers over, and we've known each other for *eons*, yet we've never actually met, as it were, in the flesh.)

Anyway, when I did log on again, I found this message in my box. "Emily Rowland. This is Selena. Care to chat?"

Well, I mean, what would you do? Seconds later I was firing
off a "Yes, please" to Selena's e-mail address. Her reply was
waiting for me when I finished up my course work that
afternoon.

"Your friend Freddy tells me you're the young woman who
won the CBC Young Composers Competition. *Suite No. 1 for
Soprano Flute and Psyche-Sounds,* I think it was?"

I was impressed. Impressed, nothing. I was so flattered and
amazed I was reduced to a babbling idiot.

"But that's . . . " I hesitated. What could I call my kind
of music, to distinguish it from Selena's Post-Gothique pop?
Was what I did Serious Music? And did that mean that
Selena's music wasn't serious? It was tough going, talking to
an international celeb. "But that's kind of different from
what you do," I finished lamely.

"Which doesn't mean I don't keep up with what's going
on in my field. And it *is* my field, Emily Rowland, make no
mistake. Selena is the future of Pyche-Music."

Well, of course, I had my own ideas about that, but I kept
them to myself.

"Listen, Emily Rowland. Do you know what an ethno-
musicologist is?"

"Of course. It's somebody who records the music of other
cultures. Native tribespeople, mostly. But I don't think they
do that any more."

"Probably not. But that's what my new project is. I want to
record the psyche-sounds of homeless children living in the
sub-levels. That's the true Gothic — the music of souls trapped
in darkness, in tunnels and bolt-holes deep in the earth."

Selena's prose style was pretty Gothic too, I noticed.

"And so?"

"And so I can't do this project alone. I need assistants —
field workers who know something about Psyche-Music, who

know how to use the equipment. Young, unthreatening people who can go down into those tunnels and move freely
among the child tribes."

The smart thing, at that moment, would have been to hit
disconnect. But this was Selena, The Queen of Darkness. I
mean, would you just hang up on the biggest pop star on holo?
So instead I flung a whole bucketful of excuses at her.

"Listen, I'm not even allowed to go to Mall Level without
an adult. If my mother knew I was prowling around in the
sub-levels, first she'd call out the Youth Cops, and then she'd
cut off my modem privileges for the next eighty-five years."

"Why does she need to know? You're a smart girl, Emily. I
can tell that already. When I was your age, I always found a way
to do what I needed to do."

I'll just bet you did, I thought. Somehow I couldn't imagine
Selena even having a mother. I could imagine her at fifteen,
though, sleeping in a black velvet nightie with RotRock posters
plastered all over the inside of her coffin.

"Plus it's really, really dangerous down there. I don't do
dangerous. People get killed in the sub-levels. Or they catch
disgusting diseases."

"They don't if they know what they're doing. I'll send you
over a little kit I've had made up. Broad-spectrum immune-
system enhancers. A stun-pistol. You'll be fine."

She was amazing, this woman. Was there anything she
hadn't thought of?

"I'll talk to Freddy," I said — while all the time a voice in
my head was screaming, "Emily, you idiot, don't do this. This
is totally insane."

Talking to Freddy was, of course, a major mistake. If Selena
had told Freddy he could fly and suggested he step out of a
window on the twenty-first level, he'd have flapped his wings
and launched himself straight off the sill.

"You want to make a career of your music, okay? Just think what working for Selena could do for you, career-wise."

I guess that's why Freddy always won, when we played computer games. He knew how to go straight for the jugular.

Selena's package arrived, as promised, by courier. Luckily my mother was at work when it dropped through our mail chute. Selena had gift-wrapped it and attached a Happy Birthday balloon, and building security had apparently let it through unchecked.

That left the question of how to get out of my tower.

"Do you ever get to go out alone?" Freddy wanted to know.

"I have a lesson at my flute instructor's once a week. But that's in our own tower, fourteen levels down."

"So, no sweat. This week you have an extra lesson — and once you're in the elevator, you just keep going. I'll meet you at the exit on Mall Level." I could tell that to Freddy this was just another holo-game, only with added special effects. (Like the chance of actually getting killed.)

* * *

I have to admit that Mall Level was a thrill. I'd been there with my mother a few times, but the idea of being alone, and able to wander around anywhere I wanted, gave me shivers up and down my spine. The scene around the elevators wasn't especially interesting — it was mid-morning, and the crowds milling around the coffee shops and boutiques were mostly business people and the odd adventurous wrinkly. There were a few of the usual teenaged cyber-weirdies with body implants and switch-blade fingernails — most people are scared of them, but I guess I looked too hopelessly nerdish to rate a second glance.

Freddy was a bit of a shock, though. It's really weird, meeting someone for real whom you've only known through the net. I'd always visualized him as tall and pale and interestingly gaunt — kind of a sixteen-year-old Edgar Allan Poe. But no, this real-life Freddy — who was closer to thirteen than sixteen — was short and barrel-shaped and chubby-cheeked. The bottom half of his face was coated with some kind of green powder — I think he hoped it would make him look cadaverous — and the top half was hidden behind purple mirrorshades. His hair, which needed washing, was frizzy and ginger-coloured. What a pair we must have made — me tall and skinny as a lamppost, wearing my favourite vintage John Lennon specs, and Freddy pumping along beside me on his little short legs, wearing those ridiculous purple shades.

To find what we were looking for we had to go a lot deeper than Mall Level, into the sub-sub levels, the service ducts and storage areas. Into Terra Incognito — the unknown country of the child tribes.

I was on safari in East Africa, I told myself, like May French Sheldon. I was Lady Hester Stanhope, riding into the desert with the Bedouins. I was the ethnologist, Daisy Bates, in the Outback, recording legends of the Dream-Time.

But first there was the question of getting down to the sub-levels. Like, we weren't exactly talking Nullabar Plain. Naturally there were armed guards on all the elevators, and the service accesses were locked and barred. But it seems that if you have as much money as Selena, you can buy just about anything. In my package, along with the other stuff she had thoughtfully provided, was a nifty little plastic access card, and a holo-map of our sector showing us where we were supposed to go, and where to use the card. It worked just fine.

"How far down are we going, anyway?" By now I was feeling pretty claustrophobic.

Freddy consulted the map. "Three levels. It's not that far down, really — there's several more levels after that, before you hit bottom."

We got off at Sub-Level Three. It was dark, and smelly, and cold, with narrow passageways going off in various directions. The ceiling lights were protected by wire screens, but nearly all the ones that hadn't burnt out were smashed. The walls were rough grey concrete, crusted over with old graffiti and unidentifiable smears. The smell seemed to get steadily worse as we moved away from the elevator. By the time we'd been walking for five minutes I felt like tossing my lunch.

I could hear Freddy beside me, his boots squelching in something I didn't really want to think about. He sounded like he was trying hard not to breathe.

We went round a corner and nearly fell over something — or somebody. I turned up the power on my hand-lamp. What had looked at first glance like a bundle of old rags on sticks was a little kid of about five — barefoot, filthy, with big spooky eyes that stared straight ahead. She was backed up against the wall of the passageway, obviously too scared to move. I could see, when I raised the lamp, that her eyes had a milky film over them. I took another step forward, and suddenly she curled up in a ball, knees pulled under her chin. All this time she was making a high squeaking noise, like a scared rabbit. Listening to that awful sound, I felt sicker than ever.

"Get the trodes on her," Freddy hissed at me.

"You dork, she's *already* petrified. If I touch her she'll totally freak."

"So?"

"Freddy, I can't believe I'm hearing this. You want me to stick this gizmo on her head, when she's all curled up like that, scared out of her wits?"

Freddy peered at me through those dumb purple shades.

"You're an observer," he said. "An anthropologist. You take notes. You record. You aren't supposed to get emotionally involved."

Meanwhile, the girl's squeals had attracted the rest of the tribe. They crept out of the shadows so quietly that before we realized what was happening they were all around us.

They didn't look dangerous, just shy and curious. The oldest couldn't have been more than eight.

They stood just out of reach, staring at us. They were really creepy, those kids. Creepy, and so pitiful that it tore your heart out by the roots. They all looked sick and half-starved, and under the layers of dirt their skin was kind of a fish-belly white, like things growing in caves — like mushrooms. A lot of them were blind, or missing parts of limbs, or with tiny little heads on normal-sized bodies. They drooled and twitched; and they kept babbling at us in what sounded *almost* like English, except that the words didn't make any sense.

My mother says it's the environment that's to blame. Nearly everyone is carrying these bent genes, she says, from all the toxins and pollutants and other guck in the air that people breathed in, before we learned to seal ourselves up in towers and never go outside without air filters and moonsuits. Okay, that's part of it. But on the science holos they teach you about natural selection and evolution and all that. And when I looked at those blind kids with their corpse-white skins, I wondered how much of it was simply adaptation to living underground. What really made me feel like puking was the idea that I might be seeing everybody's future.

One of the boys, the biggest one, seemed more or less normal, except that he had these weepy sores all over his face, and his hair grew in raggedy patches, like a crop of weeds. I figured he was the leader, so I showed him the trodes. He poked at them, ready to jump back if they tried to attack him, but at the same time he seemed fascinated by the shiny wires and the black box they were attached to.

But what clinched the deal was the bag of candy bars I pulled out of my pack. With a lot of hand signals and body language we got our message across: let us tap into your brains with these scalp-patches and shiny wires, and all these goodies are yours.

I guess this is how the tourists did it in the old days, out in the jungles, when they took 2Ds of the natives to impress their friends back home. Only we were doing it with sound. We recorded the leader first, with the monitor on, and then we played it all back to him. It was sort of harsh and jangly and ragged-edged, which is what you'd expect from the neural circuits of somebody who thought we might be planning to fry his brains. And of course raw, unsynthesized psyche-sounds are just plain noise anyway. That's the job of the psyche-musician, to turn all these bleeps and whines and squeals into something you can recognize as an art form.

Something plucked at my arm. I looked down. It was the little white rabbit-girl, staring blankly up at me. Now that the rest of the tribe had arrived, she seemed to have lost her fear. Long, spidery, bloodless fingers clutched at the folds of my coveralls.

I thought about lost kittens, abandoned puppies, needful creatures crying out for warmth and food and love. Creatures I cried about when I saw them on holo, but could do nothing to help, because in a twentieth level controlled-environment apartment they don't let you have pets.

We put the trodes on her, while she huddled against me, clinging to my hand. The noises we picked up from the mind of that starved, helpless, little creature made me want to scream, or cry, or run away. After that I turned the monitor off. I'd heard enough.

* * *

"They say there are whole gangs of kids living in the sub-levels," I said to my mother, in my most casual, I-just-happened-to-see-something-about-this-on-the-net-and-I-was-kind-of-curious voice. My mother isn't a suspicious person but she's no dummy, and if I wasn't careful a question like that could set her alarm bells off.

"Apparently so. The child tribes. I know the Youth Police have been trying to flush them out, because they get into the service ducts and the hydroponics areas, and even up into Mall Level at night."

"So where do they come from? How did they get down there?"

"Some of them are runaways, I guess. But mostly they're just the children of the homeless. There are whole families living down there, third and fourth generations. I guess when the atmosphere got really bad and everybody holed up in the towers, a lot of people had nowhere to go, so they went underground."

Next day I transmitted the tapes to Selena. I didn't listen to them. There was a message in my e-mail box next morning. "Great stuff, Emily. A really pro job. I'll send you a holo of the finished work."

* * *

I'd been reading about this totally extreme Victorian missionary called Kate Marsden, who rode thousands of miles through Siberia in the dead of winter to help the starving Russian lepers. No silk gowns and rhinestones for Kate — she nearly died herself, before she finished the trip. In the end I don't think she accomplished all that much — but she *tried*. I mean,

it was a pretty dumb stunt, when you stop to think about it —
but she really *tried*. To help. To make some difference.

I decided to send a message to Selena. I thought about it
for a long time, composing it in my head two or three different
ways before I finally sat down at the computer. It went like this.

*Selena, those kids we taped for you need decent food, and a clean
place to sleep, and medical attention. Nobody talks about them,
nobody wants to know about them. Nobody cares. Except the
Youth Cops, and they just want to keep them out of the mall. If
you'd seen them, you'd care. And you're the one person I can
think of who could make other people care. You could get your
audience to realize that what they're listening to is somebody's
hunger, and fear, and pain. And then they might do something
to help. Especially if you asked.*

I didn't get a reply right away. I didn't expect one. Selena
was busy — she had a big concert coming up in less than a
month.

* * *

I watched, of course, when Selena premiered her much-
publicized new work, The Sub-Levels Symphony. The reviews
said it was "cleverly conceived and flawlessly executed, speaking to us of the triumph of evil over good, of the terrible futility
of modern life."

Selena was artist enough to leave some of the raw edges
unsmoothed, to let the pain and hunger and hopelessness
show through. It was gritty, and real, and in places horrifying.
And yet in the end it left me untouched. And when the last
notes faded, Selena said nothing. She gave no explanation,
made no appeal. She blew a kiss to the audience and it was
over.

I couldn't leave it at that. Stupid as it sounds, I felt betrayed. For the first time I really understood the meaning of the word "exploit." Selena owed something to those children. It was their desperate, voiceless need that made her music possible. She had taken from them, and had given nothing in return.

And so I sent one final, furious message to Selena. And for some reason I still have a print-out of her reply.

Emily, sweetie, that's so tired. The sentimentality trip — the hearts and flowers stuff — it's been done to death. This is the Post-Gothique, Em. Selena is the Post-Gothique. She looks at the way the world is, with all its warts and running sores. She's an observer. She accepts the reality of evil. She doesn't try to change what is.

Somewhere I read that you shouldn't trust anybody who speaks of herself in the third person.

I never heard from Selena again.

Tourists. That's what we were. I thought of all those well-meaning Victorian lady travellers, stumping around the African jungles in their solar topees and boots and thick wool skirts, treating the natives like some kind of exotic animal, to be peered at and reported on, in the interests of scientific curiosity. I used to think they were pretty neat, those adventurous ladies. But lately I've started wondering what the natives thought, after the visitors left.

Notes on Contributors

Susan Adach is a 'writer-in-training' living in Toronto. She has held several jobs prior to this present endeavour, one of which was the promotions coordinator for the rock band Triumph. She says of "Over the Moon": "Even as a child I found the nursery rhyme 'Hey Diddle Diddle' disturbing. It was a series of actions, odd actions, but no story. The challenge here was to discover the story behind the poem from the point of view of one of its characters. Great fun, I recommend it!"
RECOMMENDED: *The Giver* by Lois Lowry.

Wayne Arthurson lives in Edmonton and is a full-time trade magazine editor and drummer for an alternative rock band. He is also a retired semi-professional clown. About "Sugar Train" he says, "Set in the Great Victoria Desert in Australia. Make your own interpretations."
RECOMMENDED: "Just read!"

Diana C. Aspin was born in Blackpool, England, and lives in Brampton, Ontario. She is a freelance writer/instructor and has been published in many magazines, journals, and newspapers across Canada. She says about writing that it is "an exploration; I have never set out to make a point. So it's always a surprise to me to discover what my story is about and that is how it was with 'Deep Freeze'."
RECOMMENDED: *The Last of the Crazy People* by Timothy Findley.

Karleen Bradford was born in Toronto, grew up in Argentina, has lived in various countries around the world, and now lives permanently in Ottawa. Bradford is published extensively in English and in translation. Her comments about "The Pig's Elbow" are: "I saw the boy in this story standing by the highway near Ottawa, where I live. I'm still not sure whether he was real or not."
RECOMMENDED: *Hexwood* by Diana Wynne-Jones.

Karin Galldin was born in Stockholm, Sweden, and is a high school student living in Ottawa. In 1994 she won a Carleton University writing contest for a non-fiction essay. About the writing of "Claire" she says, "This story is about having the courage to be an individual — don't let such an opportunity pass you by . . . ."
RECOMMENDED: *Back Home* by Michelle Magorian.

J.A. Hamilton was born in Hamilton, Ontario, and currently lives in Vancouver. Hamilton is the author of a children's book, *Jessica's Elevator,* two poetry books, *Body Rain* and *Steam-Cleaning Love,* and a volume of short fiction, *July Nights.* Her comments about the writing of "DNA" are: "Lots of people have to come to grips with absentee parents and reconstituted families — it's not easy, but it can be rewarding."
RECOMMENDED: anything by Sarah Ellis.

Linda Holeman is a full-time writer who lives in Winnipeg with her family. She has had many previous publications — in magazines and journals — and "Saying Goodbye" was awarded runner-up prize in Thistledown's 1992 national short story competition.
RECOMMENDED: *Traveling On into the Light* by Martha Brooks and *The Blue Camaro* by R.P. MacIntyre.

Jillian Horton lives in Brandon, Manitoba, and has had several publications. She says of "The Bicycle": "I wrote this story based on the premise that in our attempts to be 'like' everyone else, we often erase what is most special about us as individuals."
RECOMMENDED: *Shadow in Hawthorn Bay* by Janet Lunn.

Christine Pinsent-Johnson is an adult literacy instructor who lives in Nepean, Ontario. She has had several articles published in local magazines. About "The Visitor" she says, "It is usually the events which seem insignificant that have the most profound effects in life."
RECOMMENDED: *Some of the Kinder Planets* by Tim Wynne-Jones.

Eileen Kernaghan, a well-known young adult and speculative fiction writer, co-owns Neville Books (Burnaby, B.C.) and teaches writing courses part-time. Her publishing career spans over fifteen years, and includes novels, poetry, and short fiction. Kernaghan currently lives in New Westminster, B.C. About her story she says, " 'Tourists' is set in the world that lies just around the turn of the millenium, when technology breeds strange new forms of art, and the only safe place to travel is in cyberspace."
RECOMMENDED: *Rite of Passage* by Alexei Panshin.

S.E. Lee is a writer & illustrator living in St. Placide, Quebec.
RECOMMENDED: *The Little Country* by Charles de Lint.

Alison Lohans was born in California and immigrated to Canada in 1971. She settled in Regina in 1976, taught instrumental music for three years, then "retired" to focus on her family and her writing career. Lohans is

published extensively throughout Canada and the U.S.
Lohans says that "Peripheral Dreams" was inspired in
part by a visit to see 'Scotty', the T-rex being exhumed
near Eastend, Saskatchewan.
RECOMMENDED: *David and Jonathon* by Cynthia Voigt.

V.S. Menezes lives in Mississauga. About "Dead Jim" V.S.
Menezes says, "I grew up in a small town. I felt different
from all the other kids — and I sure dressed differently!
My fiction is about how weird and confusing the teen
years can be — especially when everyone else is so
normal."
RECOMMENDED: *The Leaving* by Budge Wilson.

Robert Morphy is an artist and writer originally from
Vancouver, now living in Toronto. About the writing of
"Comes a Time" he says, "Parents may make terrible
demands on their children in the process of seeking their
own truths. Children, as they grow, will certainly ask the
same of their elders. We may never know why our parents
chose one path over another, but we must try to understand, for ourselves, and for our own children"
RECOMMENDED: *The Leaving* by Budge Wilson and
Nightjohn by Gary Paulsen.

Jacqueline Shiromi Pinto was born in London, England,
immigrated to and grew up in Montreal, and is presently doing her M.A. in South Asian English Literature
in London, U.K.
RECOMMENDED: *A Wind in the Door* by Madelaine
L'Engle.

Terry Thulien is a veteran of Veteran, Alberta. One of Terry's interests is researching historical personalities. About "The Identity" she says, "In seeking an identity we often look in dangerous places. We covet the attention of certain people or attempt to identify with someone we think feels the same as us. Look in the right places for your identity."
RECOMMENDED: the *Cedar River Daydreams* series by Judy Baer.

Budge Wilson was born in Halifax and lives near Hubbards, Nova Scotia. She is the mother of two daughters. She has worked as a commercial artist, a freelance photographer, and a fitness instructor before starting to write full-time in 1984. Of sixteen published books, thirteen are for children and young adults. Her short story collection *The Leaving* (Stoddart 1990) has been a major national and international success. About the writing of "My War" she says, "This story was painful for me to write, and it may be painful for some of you to read. However, it often seems to me that one of the earmarks of being grown up and mature is that we start to recognize the deep gulf between the things that are romantic and sentimental and the things that are real. That is the theme of this story."
RECOMMENDED: *Paradise Café and Other Stories* by Martha Brooks.